M000227476

Systema Paradoxa

Accounts of cryptozoological import

Volume 11
Found Footage
A Tale of Mantis Man

As accounted by Mary Fan

NeoParadoxa
Pennsville, NJ
2022

PUBLISHED BY
NeoParadoxa
A division of eSpec Books
PO Box 242
Pennsville, NJ 08070
www.especbooks.com

ISBN: 978-1-949691-95-5
ISBN (ebook): 978-1-949691-94-8

Interior Design: Danielle McPhail
www.sidhenadaire.com

Cover Art: Jason Whitley
Cover Design: Mike and Danielle McPhail, McP Digital Graphics
Interior Illustration: Jason Whitley

Copyediting: Greg Schauer and John L. French

DEDICATION

FOR ALL THE KIDS WITH CAMERAS
WHO DREAM OF THE BIG SCREEN

CHAPTER ONE

Shadows mottled the forest floor, still damp from last night's rain. Being careful to avoid slipping on the leaves, Jenny Chen slid her tripod—a flimsy gray thing that refused to stand straight—forward by a few inches. She huffed as the camcorder she'd borrowed from her parents teetered, barely supported by the ill-fitting screw. *This is what I get for buying the cheapest tripod at RadioShack.* But even though she was now a high school junior, her parents had refused to up her allowance. Something about teaching her "financial responsibility."

Keeping her eyes on the minuscule screen sticking out the side of the camcorder, she did her best to straighten the picture. A stiff breeze blew her straight, black ponytail into her eyes, chilling her through her crimson zip-up sweatshirt as a cloud passed over the pale late afternoon sun. *So much for spring.* But she didn't mind the gloom—or the air of creepiness that came with it. In fact, it was just what she needed for her filmmaking project.

"It doesn't have to be perfect, you know." Standing a few yards ahead in a bright blue dress, Stacey Mandelbaum hugged her arms and nodded at the camcorder. The outfit, which Jenny had selected because it popped nicely against the brown-and-gray, not-yet-really-green forest, was a far cry from her friend's usual preference for comfortable earth tones. "You can always straighten it later when you're editing."

"'Fix it in post'? Really?" Jenny cocked an eyebrow.

"Well, if you're going to take forever, I'm putting my jacket back on. I'm freezing. Though we should hurry up and shoot the scene before it gets dark." Stacey's sharp nose and thin lips accentuated her annoyed expression. Her mature cheekbones often led people to assume she was several years older than Jenny, who, despite being seventeen, was often handed the kids' menu at restaurants.

But just because Stacey looked like she could be Jenny's teacher didn't mean she was in charge. It was Jenny's movie, and she wanted everything to be as perfect as she could make it. "Don't move. I need to frame the picture around you, and your jacket will mess up my colors."

"Fine. But you'd better not complain about anything *I* do when we shoot *my* movie next week."

Still fiddling with the tripod and camcorder, Jenny grinned. "I reserve the right to be an on-set diva. You *did* get my note about having candy dishes with only red Skittles within reach at all times, right?"

Stacey rolled her eyes.

Jenny crouched down to adjust one of the tripod's legs. Another wind blew, and the shadows grew deeper beneath the trees, which remained scraggly despite the few brave leaves unfurling from a handful of branches. A shudder ran down her spine, and she internally laughed at herself. *Guess when you make a horror movie, everything has you jumpy.*

Something rustled—a quick yet sharp fluttering noise. She jumped up, looking past Stacey in the direction of the sound.

"What?" Stacey glanced behind her.

Jenny narrowed her dark, angled eyes and looked around but found only the expected tangle of brush. "I don't know..."

Stacey put her hands on her hips. "Is this your way of getting me into character?"

Jenny shook her head. "Sorry." Ignoring an uncanny feeling of being watched, she finished adjusting her camera set-up. *I hope this scene creeps out our class as much as it's creeping me out right now.* "Okay, done." She stood and positioned herself behind the camera.

"Finally." Stacey bent her knees and put on a frightened expression.

Jenny hit the *record* button. "Rolling. Forest chase scene, take one." She waved her hand before the lens as a makeshift slate. "Action!"

Stacey ran toward the camera, a look of feigned panic in her wide brown eyes. "Don't hurt me!" She looked back, sending her loose chestnut curls flying over her shoulder, then screamed and tripped. "Please!" She dug her hands into the ground and crab-walked toward the camera. "No!" She curled up into a ball, her hands over her head.

Jenny counted silently to three. "And cut!"

Stacey stood, brushing the dirt from her dress. "How was that?"

"Pretty freaking good, actually. But this time, can you cheat your face forward when you look back?"

"Sure." Stacey returned to her mark, right next to a rock Jenny had stuck in the ground earlier.

"Also, can you—" Jenny broke off with a gasp. Something had moved—and there was no breeze this time.

Stacey whirled, then turned back to Jenny with an amused smile. "If you're trying to get me to method act, well, it's kind of working."

"Something's out there."

"'Something... from the realm beyond. Maybe a ghost... or something darker.' Did I get the lines right?"

"I'm not kidding, Stacey." That creeped-out feeling of being watched clung to Jenny as much as the cold sweat breaking against her skin. "I heard something move."

"We're in the woods. Something's always moving."

Jenny took a step forward, searching. Though the feeling remained strong, she couldn't see anything out of the ordinary. Then again, it was hard to tell with so many trees and shadows. She wasn't exactly a deer hunter or anything. "Yeah, you're right." She returned to her spot behind the camera. "Ready to go again?"

Stacey inhaled and assumed her about-to-run position. "Yup."

"Rolling... Forest chase scene, take two. Action!"

The gravel of the wide towpath along the Delaware & Raritan Canal crunched beneath Jenny's worn sneakers, which looked like crap but were too comfortable to be thrown out. Staring at the camcorder's three-inch screen, she followed Stacey back toward the parking lot.

"Can't you at least wait till we get to my car?" Stacey said. "You're gonna trip."

"Hush!" Jenny waved her off. "The auteur is at work!"

In the playback, Stacey peered out from behind a tree. The sun had been much brighter when they'd filmed that scene, and Jenny had taken so long finding the perfect spot for the chase scene and setting up for it that there was no way the audience would believe that the two moments took place within minutes of each other. *Ugh, Stacey was right. I shouldn't have been so picky.*

"What's wrong?" Stacey asked.

"What?"

"Your face is all scrunched up like you smelled dog poop. Did I miss my mark or something?"

Jenny looked up at her friend, who almost looked like a shadow under the fading light. "You were right."

Stacey stopped in her tracks and cupped her ear. "Whoa, what? Am I hearing things? Maybe there really are ghosts or demons lurking—"

Giggling, Jenny smacked the other girl. "Shut up! I can admit when I'm wrong."

"Oh, really?" The bluish-white light from the screen highlighted Stacey's skeptical expression as she leaned closer.

"Ugh, look at this." Jenny turned back to the playback, which now showed Stacey stumbling through the woods. "You can totally tell that it was filmed an hour and a half after the other scene. Also, I swear it didn't look that dark when we were shooting."

"Well, you can always adjust the brightness later and—"

"Fix it in post," Jenny finished with a slight laugh. "I guess that's why God invented editing software. Oh, and speaking of religion..." She reached into her pocket and retrieved Stacey's gold Star-of-David necklace. "Here, before I forget."

"Oh, trust me, *I* wouldn't have forgotten." Stacey took the necklace and fastened it around her neck. "I've worn my grandmother's necklace every day since first grade. I feel naked without it."

"It's been, like, twenty minutes since we wrapped. You could've reminded me sooner... you must be awfully comfortable walking around naked."

Stacey raised her hand as if to smack Jenny but froze, her eyes widening. "What was that?"

"Very funny. Is this your way of getting back at me for—"

"Rewind the playback!" Stacey reached for Jenny's camcorder, accidentally shoving her shoulder.

Already overbalanced by the tripod strapped to one shoulder and her forest-green backpack hanging off the other, Jenny landed flat on her butt, instinctively lifting the hand holding the camcorder even though that meant taking the full force of the fall. "Hey! What—?"

"There it is again!" Staring at the camcorder, Stacey pointed. "Rewind it!"

Jenny may have been the type to say *made you look*, but Stacey wasn't. And she was hardly a good enough actress to feign the startled, frightened look on her face. Jenny would know—she'd been trying to get that expression out of her friend and star all afternoon. "Okay... what's going on?"

"I don't know, but I think..." Stacey shook her head. "Just re-watch it."

Jenny hit pause and rewound at half speed. On the screen, Stacey slowly uncurled from the ground, sat up and moved into a crab-walk position, and crawled forward. It looked so creepy backward and in slo-mo that Jenny wondered if she could somehow use it for the movie—

Something flashed in the background.

"There!" Stacey cried. At the same time, Jenny hit *pause*.

Behind the tangle of shrubs, shrouded in the shadows of the trees, yet unmistakably outlined by the waning sun, stood a figure with glinting eyes. Bulbous and black—and likely only visible because of a quirk of light and digital recording technology—they stood to either side of a triangular head. A long, thin neck and body extended downward until obscured by branches, and a pair of large forelegs, angled together as if in prayer, stood before it.

If Jenny had seen the figure in a biology textbook, she would have identified it right away as a praying mantis. But... but the figure on the screen... it looked almost as big as Stacey. And it had to be several feet—no, several yards—back. Jenny may have been new at the whole filmmaking thing, but she knew how perspective worked. That figure, whatever it was, had to be at least seven or eight feet tall.

She shuddered. "I knew it... I knew there was something out there..."

"It can't have been that far from us." Stacey's voice carried a tremor. "How come we didn't see it?"

"Camouflage? Or maybe we were just too distracted?"

"Hey, if I'd known it was there when we were filming, you wouldn't have had to coach me so much about looking scared." Stacey let out a nervous laugh. "This... *isn't*... one of your pranks, is it?"

Jenny did her best to hide her fear and muster an irritated expression instead. "If it were, do you think I'd wait until *after* shooting to freak you out?"

"Fine... my turn to say it... you were right." Stacey leaned down toward the screen. "Maybe some people would try to come up with a... a rational explanation or something, but..."

"But you believe in this stuff—the stuff we can't explain." Jenny examined the image on the tiny screen. "Me too."

"I mean, I'm not going to be wearing a tin-foil hat or anything anytime soon, but I draw conclusions based on evidence." Stacey gestured at the screen. "Like *that*."

Quick, rhythmic footsteps sounded ahead. Realizing she was still on the ground, Jenny jumped up with a start. Then she recalled where they were and blew out a breath as a jogger in orange leggings came into view, a headlamp illuminating her path.

Still unsettled, Jenny barely managed to step out of the way as the jogger ran past. "Should... should we warn her that something might be out there?"

"She wouldn't believe us." Stacey twisted her mouth. "*I* hardly believe us. If I hadn't literally been there... I mean, I still don't want to believe it when I didn't see anything. It's not like we're in the middle of nowhere. This is the D&R Canal! We had to crawl through the woods for at least fifteen minutes before we found a spot that wasn't full of people. I always thought you had to be far out in the country to spot things like this."

"What is *this* anyway?" Jenny wondered what part of her had sensed the creature's presence earlier, whether she'd seen its shadow in the corner of her eye or heard its steps just a few yards before her.

Whatever it was, it was still out there. And it had been watching them.

"Let's go." Stacey marched down the towpath. "We won't find any answers out here. Looks like we have some research to do."

"Yeah, makes sense." Jenny followed, still staring at the image on the screen. She rewound a little further, and the figure vanished behind a tree for several moments. But then it peeked out again and remained until the footage cut off. Since she was watching backward, that meant it had observed them from the moment she started recording before hiding behind the tree.

How long had it lingered, mere yards away? Everything Jenny had ever seen or read about creature sightings had them fleeing the moment they were spotted. Yet this mantis had remained nearby... why? What did it want?

Even as the parking lot came into view and Stacey pressed her key to disable the alarm on her used SUV, Jenny couldn't shake the feeling that the creature still lingered, just out of sight, watching.

Between the damp branches and delicate new leaves of a tall bush, a shadow retreated into the trees. Though this place hardly counted as wilderness with so many humans nearby, the scents of dirt and rock and foliage felt feral and comfortable. But the lights—the yellow, artificial lights that flashed across the foul-smelling black pavement—they were repulsive.

Too much brightness when it should have been dark. Too much noise when it should have been silent.

Besides, the small human female had gone.

The shadow retreated.

CHAPTER TWO

Spindly black-and-brown legs covered in fine hairs tapped against the back of Jenny's hand. Smiling, she tilted her arm to let her pet tarantula crawl onto her stomach as she leaned back against her bedroom wall, her legs outstretched on the cream-colored carpet.

Sitting at Jenny's desk a few feet away, Stacey twisted away from the bulky desktop monitor, which was nice enough for used tech but seemed clunky compared to the sleek flat-screen monitors Jenny had seen at her parents' workplaces.

"Hey," Stacey said. "Correct me if I'm wrong, but last time I checked, Mulder the Tarantula didn't know how to enhance digital film."

"Maybe not, but he's good at making me feel better for wasting a whole hour because I didn't know what I was doing." Jenny scooped up the fuzzy five-inch-long arachnid and stood. Her knee brushed against her heavy black laptop, which was connected to the camcorder on the floor beside her by a thick wire. She grimaced. "I've tried everything, but nothing's helping. Maybe this free editing software just isn't good enough. Whatever that thing in the woods was, it appears in several frames, but I can't make out any more details than what we saw on the camcorder's screen."

"Join the club." Stacey glanced at the desktop monitor. "I've scoured every website and forum I could find, and as far as I can tell, there's no lore about a giant praying mantis. Or if there is, it must be on a site too obscure for me to find. It's not like we spotted Bigfoot or something."

"Well, this sucks." Jenny lightly traced one finger across her tarantula's back.

Stacey recoiled. "Can you put that thing back in its tank?"

"What, don't you want to pet him?" Jenny shoved out her hands, moving Mulder closer to Stacey.

Stacey swatted at the air. "Stop it!"

Laughing, Jenny retreated and approached the clear ten-gallon tank on the bottom shelf of her bookcase. "You know he's harmless!"

"Sure, but he still creeps me out."

"Thought you liked the weird? You never complain on movie nights when I pick creature films."

"That's different—those are *movies*. That's a giant *spider*." Stacey gestured emphatically at the tarantula.

"Hey, be nice to my baby." Jenny gently lowered her pet—which she'd only told her parents about after the tank was all set up and it was too late for them to say no—into the habitat she'd lovingly crafted out of the best materials Petco had to offer. She'd saved her birthday, Christmas, and Chinese New Year money for a whole year to buy the tarantula and everything it needed to thrive, and she'd convinced Stacey to drive her to the store. Green plastic leaves crowded over fake rocks. She gave Mulder a wistful look as he settled down beside the toy skull in the corner. "Someday, I'll get you a real terrarium with real plants. You'd like that, wouldn't you?" She turned back to Stacey. "Speaking of giant bugs, maybe we should trade jobs. You try to enhance the image of the mantis, and I'll search the web for lore."

Stacey glanced at her watch. "Maybe tomorrow. It's getting late, and I don't want to have to speed to get home on time."

"Thought you didn't have a curfew?"

"Not from my parents, but the great State of New Jersey thinks I'll turn into a pumpkin if I drive after midnight." Stacey rolled her eyes. "Can't wait until I can finally graduate from this Cinderella license."

"Oh, right. Forgot about that."

"Not surprised since you refuse to even get your permit."

"The idea of driving freaks me out, okay? I mean, I once totaled my bicycle! Besides, living in university housing means everything's within walking distance."

Stacey got up from the chair. "Sometimes, I wish my dad worked at the university just so he could give me the discarded tech. I still can't believe you have *two* computers."

"Don't be too jealous. That desktop is so old, I'm pretty sure it's going to explode one of these days."

As Jenny went to pick up the laptop, she glimpsed the desktop monitor and the last forum Stacey had been searching: a poorly designed site professing to chronicle cryptid sightings in the Tri-State Area. "Maybe if we check back in a few days, someone else will have spotted the mantis and posted about it... or maybe we should post what we found, and someone will say something?"

Stacey shook her head. "I don't think we should go putting things on the internet when we barely know what's going on. People probably won't believe us... heck, *I* hardly believe us. I just don't want to look like an idiot."

"I guess maybe we should at least wait until we have better footage." Jenny crouched on the floor and closed the laptop, which had displayed her latest fruitless effort to make the shadow look more like... something more than a shadow. "I'm going to go to Mr. Fernando tomorrow after school and see if he has any suggestions. Maybe just using the professional editing software in the computer lab will help."

"Good idea."

"After that... can you give me a ride to the canal? The spot where we were today, I mean?" Jenny gave her friend a pleading grin. "I mean, I could bike, but it's kind of far."

Stacey crossed her arms. "Are you a monster hunter now, Jenny?"

"I just want to see if there's anything we missed!"

"What, like maybe the oversized praying mantis left a note?"

"I don't know." Jenny twisted her mouth. "I just know it's out there, and there's got to be something more to find."

"And what will you do if you find it? Wave hello and ask it to come over for dinner? You'd probably be the main course." Stacey gave Jenny an exasperated look. "It's not like Mulder, Jenny. It's probably dangerous. Not to mention *enormous*. We probably got lucky today... maybe it didn't like the odds of two against one."

Jenny jittered, tapping one hand against the other. When she realized it, she forced her hands still. Though the idea of an eight-foot-tall mantis watching her still creeped her out, her curiosity was stronger than her fear. If Stacey knew, she'd never agree to help. But Jenny would rather confront her fears than let go of the most exciting mystery in her life.

"I have to know what it is," she muttered. "I have to know why it was watching us, what it wanted, where it came from. It was *right there*, and we didn't see it. I don't want to go the rest of my life not knowing."

Stacey's lips twitched. "You can be such a drama queen sometimes."

"Hey, isn't that why we make movies? For the drama?" Jenny arched her brows. "So, will you give me a ride?"

"Fine, but only because I don't like the idea of you searching for a giant mantis alone... on a bike! I'll try to swipe my mom's pepper spray... I wonder if that stuff would work on the creature."

"Now who's being the drama queen?" Jenny grinned. "Thanks."

"I'd better let my mom know I'm on my way home." Stacey grabbed her backpack, unzipped its smallest pocket, and retrieved a chunky silver flip phone. "I'll see you in school tomorrow."

The computer lab was empty when Jenny arrived. Figuring Mr. Fernando was probably on his way, she went ahead and settled down at one of the desktops.

Her backpack dropped like a sack of rocks when she set it down, and she panicked for a moment, fearing she might have damaged the camcorder. But it was fine — not even a single new scratch despite having spent the whole school day rubbing up against her textbooks, binders, and notebooks — and soon, she had it plugged into a computer. It took a while for the footage to transfer — maybe it was a good thing Mr. Fernando was late — but once it did, pulling it up in an editing program was a matter of a few clicks.

For what had to be the hundredth time, she re-watched what her camera had captured: the towering shadow with a triangular head and the menacing forelegs, tucked between tangled branches, dark yet unmistakable behind Stacey. Jenny wondered if, when she enhanced the image, she'd find spikes on those forelegs like those of an actual praying mantis. If so, they'd probably be the size of daggers.

Why did it appear, hide, and then reappear? What was it waiting for? Between its first and second appearances, a few minutes had passed. But Jenny recalled that feeling of being watched the entire time they'd been filming. How much had been her imagination, and how much had been some kind of primitive instinct, warning her that there was a possible predator nearby?

The door to the computer lab opened, and a broad-shouldered man with a neat black beard and copper-toned skin entered.

Jenny jumped up from her seat. "Mr. Fernando!"

He approached with a friendly smile. "Jenny Chen. I should have known I'd find you here. So, what help does your masterpiece need today?"

"This is a little different, actually. My camcorder captured something in the woods yesterday evening, and I was hoping to enhance the image to find out more about what it is. But nothing I tried at home worked. Of course, I'll admit, free software sucks."

"Well, let's see what we can do." Mr. Fernando grabbed a chair and wheeled it over. "What exactly are you hoping to achieve?"

"See that?" Jenny pointed at the silhouetted creature on the monitor. "I want a better look so I can figure out what it is."

Mr. Fernando adjusted his glasses. "Maybe it's my eyesight, but I don't see what you're talking about. It just looks like forest vegetation under shifting light."

"That's why I need to enhance it!"

Mr. Fernando chuckled. "Okay, okay. Let me try something."

Jenny pushed against the edge of the table, sending her chair wheeling backward to give Mr. Fernando space.

For the next few minutes, her filmmaking teacher clicked through the editing program, causing the image on the screen to grow larger, brighten, and shift colors based on his commands. But the shadow remained featureless. No new details emerged, and no clues appeared from the darkness.

"I'm sorry, Jenny, but I really don't know what you're looking for." Mr. Fernando moved his chair aside to give her room to return. "All I see are shrubs and shadows."

"You don't see the giant mantis?" Jenny circled it with her finger. "It's—It's right there!"

Mr. Fernando narrowed his eyes at the screen. "I guess from a certain angle, it does look like a bug. Then again, so does this cluster here." He pointed at a shadow on a different section of the screen. "If you squint, it looks a little like a head with antennae."

Jenny shook her head and shuddered. "This one's different."

"Hey, if people can photograph the Loch Ness Monster or the Jersey Devil or what have you, then there's no reason to doubt that this *could* be a giant mantis." An amused gleam lit Mr. Fernando's brown eyes. "If you're hoping to use that as an effect for your movie project, then I say go for it."

"I'm *serious*. I... I know what I saw!"

Mr. Fernando's expression turned to sympathy. "I can see you had a frightening experience, and I'm sorry about that. I suggest that the next time you film, try to stay closer to the path, and maybe choose a brighter time of day. I don't want the school board to think I'm sending students into the woods or that by letting you make any movie of your choice — including horror — I'm making you vulnerable to trauma."

"I'm not—" Jenny broke off. "Never mind. Thanks anyway."

"I'm sorry I couldn't be more helpful. I look forward to seeing your project when it's done." He got up.

Jenny ejected her camcorder from the computer, packed up her things, and left the lab, heading for the library where Stacey had said she'd do her homework while she waited.

A new determination coursed through Jenny. She *would* find more evidence of the mantis-like creature that evening. Or if not, she'd come back the next evening. And after that, it would be the weekend, and she could spend all day searching.

That sounded stupid, even in her head. Stacey would certainly call her a drama queen again if she knew what Jenny was thinking. But Jenny was certain of what she'd seen, and she had to prove it. And while what she caught on tape was good enough for Stacey, it probably wouldn't convince anyone else.

I need something good... I need people to know. She marched past the dented lockers and brick walls of Princeton High School, her thoughts churning.

Blood exploded as the creature's forelegs dug into the flesh of its prey. The helpless other wriggled uselessly in the creature's grasp, grasped by a force too powerful for its puny body to resist.

A beaklike mouth pressed against its victim, and pincers extended to suck out an eye. Juices spilled as the creature ate and ate. The prey thrashed. If it could have emitted a sound, surely its scream would have reverberated through the woods.

CHAPTER THREE

Leaves crackled beneath a waning sun. Jenny had never been under any illusions that she could sneak up on the mantis — if indeed it was still out there — but still she wished her canvas shoes didn't make such a racket. Branches swayed with the breeze, and a few strands from her ponytail tickled the back of her neck.

She held her camcorder out before her as she imagined a hunter would carry a rifle. A red light blinked along the side of its silver casing, telling her that the battery was low. She was probably running out of space on her tape as well. Maybe filming her every step hadn't been the most efficient option, but it was her best chance of capturing something more detailed this time.

She lifted the device and looked through the viewfinder, scanning. Everything looked darker on camera. Maybe that was why she hadn't been able to turn her last footage into something that could convince others of what she'd seen.

A shadow with curly hair came into the frame, and another crunching sound floated through the cool spring air. Jenny looked away from the camera to find Stacey approaching, her own camcorder out beside her.

"Ready to call it a day?" Stacey said in an annoyed tone.

Jenny glanced at her watch and then up at the twilit sky, just visible between the fluttering tree branches. "Let's give it another few minutes. Maybe the creature is nocturnal, and being out later will increase our chances of finding it."

"No." Stacey pressed a button on her camcorder, which emitted a soft beeping noise to indicate that it was shutting down. "We've come out here every day for a week, and we haven't found anything. Meanwhile, you still haven't finished filming your movie, and we were supposed to start mine the day before yesterday, remember? But instead, we're out here hunting for something that no one else believes exists. I don't want to flunk filmmaking class because of it. More than that, I *do* want to make my movie, and I don't think it's fair that I might not get to because you're obsessed with this thing."

"We'll be fine! We already got most of the stuff for my movie, and we still have plenty of time to film yours."

"Okay, so can we start tomorrow?" Stacey shoved her fists into her hips, creasing the olive-green corduroy. "Or will you insist on coming out here again if you don't find your shadow?"

"It's not *my* shadow. You're the one who spotted it on my camcorder last week and called it evidence."

"Yeah, well, that was before I knew you were going to drag me out here every day and waste our time crawling through the woods when we have other stuff to do." Stacey tucked her camcorder into its bag, which hung across her amber Henley shirt on a wide black strap. "This has gotten ridiculous. Yes, I believe there was something out here, but I don't think it's worth it to keep searching when that's gotten us nowhere. What are you trying to prove, anyway? Thought you wanted to be a movie director, not a cryptozoologist."

"That's a thing you can be? Like, professionally?" With a small smile, Jenny shook her head. "I don't know what it is about this mantis creature... I just have to find it. I know it's real, and it's the most amazing thing I've ever been close to. I mean, we might have discovered a whole new species, and I can't prove it, even though I have it on tape!"

"So, are you going to become one of those people who dedicate their whole lives to chasing one thing? Look, there's nothing wrong with being determined, but... *every day*, Jenny. At the expense of your movie project—and mine!"

"Hey, I had to read *Moby Dick* too. I'm not becoming Captain Ahab, I promise. I just think that the longer we wait, the less likely we are to find it. Who knows, in a couple of weeks, it could be all the way in Pennsylvania."

"It could be in Pennsylvania now!" Stacey zipped up her camcorder bag, and any trace of humor vanished from her eyes. "I'm done with this, Jenny. It was fun for a few days, but I have a life. If you want to keep searching, well, that's your problem. I'm going home. Call your parents if you need a ride."

"C'mon, Stacey." Jenny lowered her chin and pursed her lips in an exaggerated pout. "Let's keep looking until the end of this week. We can cover twice as much ground with both of us at it, and... well... it's more fun with you here."

"I'm sorry, I can't. Because of this whole thing, I had to ask for an extension on my history paper, and I haven't even started getting the props together for my movie. I don't want to ditch you or anything, but... but to be honest, you're being kind of selfish. And I'm done with it." Stacey turned away and marched back toward the towpath.

Jenny didn't know how to reply. She watched in silence as her friend disappeared from sight. A swirl of emotions wound through her — annoyance, anger, and sorrow all at once. Stacey was supposed to be the practical one, and she'd admitted to seeing the creature. How could she not understand that the best window to capture its image again was *right now*? More than that, how could she go off in the middle of the woods and leave Jenny alone and stranded?

Yet, at the same time, guilt crept up Jenny's heart. She'd definitely been neglecting her project because she'd been so busy looking for the creature, and Stacey had a point about it being unfair that she was behind on her own film.

Just until the end of the week, Jenny told herself. *Then I'll stop looking, even if I don't find anything.*

She continued through the woods alone, still holding her camcorder before her. She suddenly realized that the device had captured her entire argument with Stacey, and heat rushed up to her cheeks. *I'll have to delete all that before anyone can stumble across it. Ugh, that'll be cringe-y, having to watch some of it again to make sure I only delete the parts I want to.* But even as she thought that she knew she'd comb through the background first, just in case there was any sign of the mantis.

Branches tapped against each other as another breeze passed. Shadows stretched and yawned under the darkening sky. Jenny shivered, suddenly aware of how isolated she truly was. Her breaths and footsteps were the only sounds around other than the whisper of the wind and the occasional rustle caused by a squirrel or a rabbit.

She'd never been out in the wilderness by herself before, and it comforted her to know that this wasn't *actually* "the wilderness." Nearly nothing in Central Jersey qualified as that. Even if she got lost, all she'd have to do was pick a direction and keep going straight long enough to hit the towpath, a hiking trail, or a street.

Yet a cold shard of fear remained embedded in her chest as she pressed on, camcorder at the ready. *Where are you, Mantis?*

Something snapped in the distance. Jenny whipped around. Another snapping noise rang out, followed by a few more. She tensed. Was something approaching? She suddenly wished she'd grown up in the country or something so she might have recognized normal, safe sounds, oh, when she found herself abandoned in a forest with night fast descending.

The noises continued, and soon, a low hum joined it. There was something artificial about the noise; it certainly didn't sound like anything an animal or person could make. Yet she didn't recognize its mechanical whir, though she didn't exactly know a lot about machinery. *Add "construction worker's kid" to the list of things I wish I'd grown up as. Dang, having a chemistry professor for a dad and a finance exec for a mom is certainly useless when it comes to survival-type skills.*

Part of her wanted to dismiss the noises as just... noises. Maybe home construction in the distance, or road repair work. Again, there was no real "wilderness" around. Humans had to be behind the sounds. But they'd been doing enough construction at her school that she knew exactly what a power saw or jackhammer sounded like. And that unnatural hum was nothing close.

Mustering up her courage, Jenny took a step in the direction of the noise, standing on tiptoe in hopes of being near silent. No such luck— her step was as loud as any.

But nothing changed in the rhythm of the snapping or humming, so she could only guess that whatever was making the sounds hadn't heard her.

She took another step, holding her camcorder out before her like a shield. If something... unusual... happened ahead, she wanted to capture it.

Another shade of darkness wafted across the ground. Soon, she'd have to use the small flashlight attached to her keychain to see. Then there'd be no hope of remaining undetected.

Jenny had never considered herself afraid of the dark, but the encroaching shadows turned her blood to rivers of ice.

She was in the middle of nowhere, and it was getting really, really dark. Never mind that this was safe, little Princeton, New Jersey—or technically right outside the township's borders. For one eleventh grader to be out by herself without any sign of human life or occupation nearby was scary as all heck.

Jenny pressed ahead. Even if whatever made that noise had nothing to do with the mantis, she wanted to know what was going on. If it turned out to be construction, she'd laugh at herself and go home. *Yeah, that's the plan. Let's just see what's going on, then go back to the towpath. I'll bet Stacey didn't actually leave — she's probably sitting in her car in the parking lot, doing her homework and waiting for me to come back so she can say "I told you so" when I don't have anything to show.*

The thin foliage of a spring that hadn't quite yet blossomed moved like dancers around Jenny. With each step, she felt the impending night pressing harder — and her desire to leave grew stronger.

An uncanny feeling tiptoed up her spine — the feeling of being watched, same as the evening she'd filmed her forest chase scene with Stacey. Did that mean the creature was close once again? Or was it paranoia?

Then, she saw it: The shadow with a triangular head and powerful, bent forelegs. And this time, she was close enough to see that they *were* spiked like those of a regular praying mantis.

It couldn't have been more than fifteen feet in front of her, and yet all she could see was the outline. Too much vegetation and darkness obscured the rest. But was it enough?

She stared, frozen, her camcorder still rolling.

The shadow stared, motionless, its bulging eyes still watching.

In fact, it remained so statue-like, Jenny almost wondered if she was blinking at a sculpture. Only that unnamable yet unmistakable feeling in her gut told her that she was looking at a living thing and that its eyes stared into hers.

She felt it reaching into her thoughts. She couldn't explain it — she just knew it was looking inside her mind, her soul, even. She sensed it poking around in her head, though she had no idea what it was searching for. It wasn't as if she heard voices. More like a presence, occupying her brain alongside her own consciousness, probing with the dexterity of a surgeon.

Who are you? she wondered. *What do you want from me? Can you hear my thoughts? Can you answer me?*

The forest shuddered under a chilling gust, and enough branches bent across the creature to obscure it entirely. When the wind settled down, and the branches returned to their resting places, the shadow was gone.

Jenny remained frozen. Her breathing shook, partly out of awe and partly out of sheer, unadulterated terror.

She'd found what she was looking for, all right. It was time to go—yet she couldn't move.

Come on, just take a step! Gritting her teeth, she forced herself to straighten her posture. That was a start. She began to turn away, but some instinct pulled her forward instead. Maybe the creature was still there... it had appeared and reappeared in her last video, after all. Maybe she had a chance at a better look...

Something crashed through the foliage, large and dark and threatening. She whirled, camcorder up. A black figure, too obscured for her to make out even its general shape, lunged at her, and a scream ripped from her throat.

Her feet took off running before her mind had a chance to even consider what to do. She ran as hard as she could, stumbling between shrubs and over rocks.

Too close—the human came too close. But the trees were too thick, the ground too uneven. The creature crashed through the woods, anything but elegant in his movements. He rushed on legs powerful enough to carry him forward at an alarming speed. Yet, the actions were clumsy. This was not what he had been built for. He was an ambush predator, not a chase predator.

But if the human wanted a chase, he would chase.

CHAPTER FOUR

When did it get so dark? Why didn't I bring something to cut through all this brush? And why on earth did I ever think it was a good idea to cheat in PE class? Until now, Jenny had never regretted hiding behind the high jump mat instead of running around the track like she was supposed to. She'd never been sorry for her inability to jump over a hurdle without knocking it over or navigate between cones without tripping at each turn.

Then again, she'd never thought she'd find herself crashing through the woods with scarcely a spattering of light left in the sky, running from an eight-foot-tall attacker.

She wished she could reach for the mini flashlight attached to her keychain, but that was zipped up in her backpack, and she wasn't stupid enough to stop to dig it out. She'd seen enough horror movies; she knew how things like that usually ended. Even if she wanted to try grabbing it without stopping, she didn't have enough hands. Her right remained wrapped around her camcorder, and her left shielded her face from smashing into every springy branch and cluster of leaves she plunged through.

She ran a few steps to the left, then abruptly switched directions and turned right, weaving around a tree trunk. Somewhere in the recesses of her memories, she recalled watching an episode of *Kratt's Creatures* or something as a kid that described how antelope ran from predators in a zigzag because that made them harder to catch. She hadn't exactly intended on using a prey's strategy—with all the brush in the way, she couldn't have run in a straight line if she'd wanted to—but she hoped it at least helped.

With any luck, her haphazard fleeing would take her to a road or a path soon. *No real wilderness in Princeton, right? C'mon, where's a busy street when you need one?* If she could just make it somewhere with other people, surely the creature would give up its chase. It'd been so good about avoiding others before...

Her lungs screamed at her for abusing them so, and her legs burned from being used in ways they weren't used to. If only she hadn't let her high school sport be marching band — playing the clarinet. If only she'd actually given a crap about physical stuff before her life depended on it —

Her foot caught on something, and she crashed to the ground. A startled scream escaped her, and the camcorder tumbled out of her grasp. She instinctively jumped up but then froze.

Wait... where'd it go? Other than her own ragged breathing, she couldn't hear anything nearby. Nothing resembling footsteps or the inevitable noises that a giant bug would make crashing through the foliage. Come to think of it, a creature that big should have already caught up to her; no way could she have outrun it.

Yet she didn't detect any sign that the mantis was nearby, and that uncanny sensation in her gut was absent. *Maybe it gave up? Thought I wasn't worth its time? Huh, I'm almost insulted...*

Her pulse pounded like a jackhammer. She looked around, though that seemed like a useless thing to do when the sky had been reduced to a few deep blue flecks between the branches.

She wanted to tell herself that she'd gotten away, that she could relax a bit and just worry about finding the towpath. But an uncomfortable feeling remained, warning her not to become complacent, and she soon realized why.

Praying mantises were ambush predators — she remembered learning that from a nature video in biology class, which had also depicted one eating a fly alive. She had no way of knowing if that behavior applied to the mysterious creature that resembled a giant version of one, but... what if it did? What if the reason she couldn't detect anything was because the mantis waited for her to draw close enough? It had jumped out at her before, after all, right when she'd thought it was safe to move.

She remained frozen where she stood, too frightened to even search for her fallen camcorder or retrieve her mini flashlight. Tears of panic stung her eyes. *I'm such an idiot... I should've left with Stacey...*

A strange, low whirring noise emitted in the distance. It was the same sound she'd heard previously, the one whose source she couldn't identify. Her breathing shook, and her gaze darted around. What *was* that? Did it have anything to do with the creature?

The sound grew deeper, shifting from an even hum to a wide pulse. There was something unmistakably mechanical about it, and it seemed to reverberate in her very bones. But it didn't sound any closer than before, not that she could tell.

For what felt like an eternity, she remained rooted where she stood, hardly daring to even move her head. She kept expecting that any moment, something would jump out again, and terror spiraled through her. She wasn't sure how she'd been lucky enough to evade her attacker's grasp last time, but she wasn't counting on that good fortune to repeat itself.

The whirring went on, but otherwise, the woods remained still.

The mantis might still be waiting in ambush, but Jenny couldn't stand there forever. Especially since what little daylight that had been left was nearly gone.

She slowly shifted her backpack to hang off one shoulder, then unzipped the pocket holding her keys. She winced at the clinking noises they made as she pulled them out. She felt between them for the small round shape of her mini flashlight and pressed the end to turn it on.

The whirring stopped. Alarmed, she switched the light off. She must have just turned herself into a beacon, the one source of light within eyeshot. Whatever was making the whirring noise might have spotted her. But what would it want with her?

Once again, she stood frozen. *Come on, Jenny! You have to get out of here!*

If she'd made herself visible, it was already too late. The least she could do was attempt to get away. She tentatively switched the light back on. Holding her breath, she panned it along the ground until its dim, yellowish beam fell on her camcorder. She crouched down as quietly as she could. Maybe all this caution was useless when it would hardly make a difference if the mantis *were* waiting to ambush her, but she didn't feel right carelessly stomping around either.

She picked up the device. The battery was low, but it was still recording. *Maybe it captured that weird sound... I wonder what that could have been.* Though she considered putting it in her backpack, she decided she'd rather hold out hope of capturing more on video.

With her light out before her, she made her way forward. She still had no idea where she was going, but hopefully, she'd come across some sign of civilization soon.

Leaves and twigs crackled beneath her footsteps. Sweat dripped down her forehead, and tension squeezed her chest like a huge invisible fist.

The whirring noise started up again. She stopped in her tracks. It sounded louder this time... did that mean its source was closer?

If it did have something to do with the mantis, and if the creature was out there and meant to attack her, then she was doomed. There was no place to hide, and standing still seemed like a surefire way to get caught.

It was fight or flight. And while she was no good at either, she decided she'd rather take her chances on flight.

She stumbled through the woods as fast as she could, trying not to think about the possibility of an ambush ahead. The whirring continued, swirling relentlessly in her ears. And it kept crescendoing...

It hit her that she might actually be running toward its source without realizing it. She'd assumed it was coming from too far away to matter—an idiotic thing to do, in hindsight.

She switched directions and ran. But the noise grew louder still. It seemed to be coming from all directions at once. *How's that possible? Am I surrounded?*

A blue light broke the shadows ahead of her, small but piercing. She gasped and stopped so abruptly, she stumbled to her knees. A second light appeared beside it, and the two bright pinpoints danced between the far-off trees.

Curiosity gnawed at her, but she warned herself that she was in enough trouble as it was without investigating strange lights. Curiosity had gotten her ambushed by a mysterious mantis creature, after all.

She picked herself up and ran in the opposite direction. Rustling noises sounded from ahead, and third blue light appeared directly before her.

A yelp of surprise ripped from her throat, and she shifted directions once more. She just had to keep going no matter what, had to flee as fast as she could for any chance at escape—

A figure stepped out before her. Before she could react, something seized her shoulders, and she cried out in panic.

"Jenny! Jenny, it's me!"

The light from Jenny's flashlight spilled onto Stacey's face. Jenny blinked in shock, then exhaled in relief. "What—What are you doing here?"

"Looking for you, of course!" Stacey released Jenny's shoulders, an alarmed look creasing her brows. "I was nearly back to the towpath when I heard you scream, and I turned right around. My flashlight died, though. What happened?"

Jenny swallowed hard. "We have to leave. It's still out there—can't you hear that?"

Stacey furrowed her brows. "The humming, you mean?"

"Yeah. I can't figure out where it's coming from, but I heard it right before the mantis appeared—"

"You saw it again?" Frightened surprise filled Stacey's tone.

Jenny nodded. "It-it was right in front of me. And I could tell it was... reading me. It was in my head. And then it jumped out at me, but I got away. I don't know if this sound has anything to do with it, or the lights."

"There were lights too?" Stacey gripped Jenny's arm. "Never mind, we'll talk about it later. Let's get out of here before... before something happens."

Jenny nodded again and followed Stacey between the trees. The whirring noise broke off. Jenny looked around nervously. "What do you think that was?"

"No idea." Stacey glanced at the camcorder. "Did you know you're still recording?"

"Oh, right." Jenny considered turning the device off but changed her mind. "I'll let it keep running... just in case."

A frightened look filled Stacey's brown eyes. "You don't think we'll come across it again, do you?"

"I don't know."

The humans were near—so near, the creature could easily have snapped off one's head with his powerful forelegs if he wanted to. But ambushing them would do no good when there was more than one, and he could only attack them individually, giving the other a chance to become a threat. He would not take the risk—he was not desperate enough yet.

And so, the shadowed figure remained where he stood, as still as the trees surrounding him, indistinguishable from them in the darkness.

CHAPTER FIVE

Strange bluish-white pinpricks floated across the camcorder's screen, but the low whirring noise Jenny had heard was barely audible in the recording. Though she and Stacey had made it to the SUV several minutes ago, Jenny's pulse remained a thumping mess in her veins. She felt bad about all the sweat that had to be dripping off her and getting Stacey's passenger seat all gross.

Though Stacey sat behind the steering wheel, her engine remained off—and her interior lights on. A frightened look filled her face as she peered over at the camcorder. "That's freaky."

"It didn't quite capture everything." Jenny furrowed her brow. "That noise was a lot... I don't know... deeper?"

"I remember it wasn't loud, but you could feel it in your core. Like a sub-woofer or something. Your microphone probably wasn't sensitive enough to pick up something like that."

The video continued rolling. Jenny had lost track of which part of her desperate race through the woods she'd gotten to. All the spinning and blurring shadows looked the same, interrupted only by flashes of those odd lights. There must have been moments when she'd been looking in a different direction than the camcorder because the lights showed up a lot more often than she remembered seeing. "This can't be a coincidence," she muttered.

Stacey fiddled with her necklace. "You said you felt like the creature was reading your mind, right?"

"Not just my mind—it was reading *me*. As if it wanted to know more than what I was thinking... it wanted to know who I was."

"Interesting..." Stacey hesitated. "Your camera was rolling when you encountered it? Can you rewind back to that?"

Jenny nodded, though part of her wanted to say no. For some reason, the thought of looking at the mantis again made her uncomfortable. But that was ridiculous—the whole point of this adventure had been for her to encounter the creature, and she'd succeeded.

She pressed the button to rewind, watching jagged shadows leap across the screen until she reached a part where they didn't move so much, indicating that she'd been standing still. She then went forward and backward in the footage, using the camcorder's slow-motion feature, until she found the shot of the mantis.

Even half an inch tall on the screen, something about it still seemed menacing. Though it was barely visible—with its brown-and-black body virtually blending into the forest behind it and the dimness from the waning day obscuring any details—the sight of it still made Jenny shiver.

"It was right in front of me." She turned the camcorder so Stacey could get a better look. "I saw it as clearly as I see you, but that's not coming across in the video."

"Seems clear enough to me..." Stacey trailed off, a disturbed look in her eyes.

"What is it?"

Stacey shook her head. "It's ridiculous. You'll make fun of me."

"Just tell me!"

Stacey glanced at the screen again, then back at Jenny. "Okay... like I said, it sounds ridiculous, but... have you noticed that a mantis head... kind of looks the same as a gray alien's?"

Jenny arched her brows. "You mean like in Roswell?"

"Yes, exactly."

"You're right... that sounds ridiculous."

"And a giant mantis is somehow more plausible than an alien?" A sarcastic smile twisted Stacey's mouth. "I never thought I'd find myself arguing over things that shouldn't exist, but just think about it for a moment. Both times you saw the creature, it was getting dark out, and the camera didn't exactly capture all the details. Maybe what we thought were mantis arms was actually something else, and maybe we assumed it was a mantis because we were in the woods, and woods mean bugs. But all those strange noises we heard, the floating lights... doesn't that seem more sci-fi flick than monster movie to you?"

A sudden laugh escaped Jenny. "Maybe we've been watching too many of both. That's what the cops would say if we told them."

"*When* we tell them." Stacey turned to face her steering wheel. "I'm driving us to the police station. And don't argue—I've already made up my mind. You should turn off your camcorder. You're practically out of power as it is, and they might ask to see the video more than once." She set her jaw with determination and started the SUV.

Jenny closed the camcorder screen and shut off the device. "This is a bad idea, Stacey. They'll only laugh at us."

"Then they'll be the ones at fault, not us, if that thing attacks someone else. I don't feel right pretending nothing happened when there's an inexplicable creature lurking near the towpath. People are always walking and biking and jogging there—what if it gets bolder and decides to strike at a family out for an afternoon stroll?"

Jenny nodded, shuddering. It *had* tried to attack her, after all. But something felt... wrong. Twice the creature had been right in front of her and *not* attacked. Why had it vanished, only to come at her again from the side? Why hadn't it simply lunged forward? *Nothing makes sense right now. Maybe the cops will have some idea of what to do, though I doubt it.*

She put on her seatbelt as Stacey pulled out of the parking lot.

The officer glared between Jenny and Stacey with unamused gray eyes. "Very funny, girls. Where's Ashton Kutcher?"

Jenny tilted her head. "Huh?"

"You know, the new MTV show where they prank people with hidden cameras. Isn't that what you kids are watching these days?"

Jenny wanted to say, *Well, these particular kids are nerds who watch* X-Files *and* Star Trek *reruns and who barely know what MTV is.* But she had a feeling that admitting to liking paranormal and sci-fi stuff would only hurt her case when she was trying to prove that something real had happened. She shoved the camcorder, which was paused on a still of the mantis—or alien, or whatever it was—across the officer's desk. "This isn't a joke. Just *look*. It's right there."

The officer leaned back in his chair. "Nice prop. You're committed, that's for sure. But if you're hoping that *Town Topics* will run a head-line tomorrow saying there's been a mysterious monster sighted near the D&R Canal and the Princeton Police Department is warning people to stay away, then I'm afraid I'm going to have to disappoint you. I don't know if you're doing this prank on a dare or just for attention, but whatever's going on, I suggest you stop before you get yourselves in real trouble. Lying to the police is no joking matter."

"We're telling the truth!" Stacey gave him an indignant look. "My dad's a lawyer—I know you're not supposed to lie to the police! If this were a prank, I'd be the first to kill it. But I came here—and I *made* Jenny come here—because I'm more worried about peoples' safety than looking stupid."

The officer lifted one bushy brown eyebrow. "Now, correct me if I'm wrong, but didn't you say it was Jenny here that spotted the thing? Both times?"

"Yes, but—"

"And you only saw the playback, right?"

"Well, yes."

The officer turned to Jenny. "So, it sounds like it's only your word we have, and your friend implied that you didn't really want to tell the authorities about what you encountered. You said you were in the woods in the first place because you were shooting a horror movie for a school project, isn't that right?"

Jenny realized where the officer was going with his rhetorical questions, and she scowled. "Stacey's been my best friend since sixth grade. I wouldn't lie to her just to make a movie."

"How sweet." The officer's tone was flat. "Whatever you're hoping to pull, it won't work. Now, you girls should go home. It's a school night, after all."

Jenny stood. "Fine." She reached for the camcorder, but Stacey caught her arm.

"Just look at it again, officer." Stacey gave the middle-aged man a pleading look. "What if we're right, and someone gets hurt? You'd warn people if there was a feral bear or something near the towpath, wouldn't you?"

"Bears are real. Bigfoot here isn't." The officer gestured at the camcorder. "Or Big Mantis."

"But—"

"Look here, kid, I've been patient, but you're wearing me down. I'm not stupid enough to believe in the unexplained or paranormal or whatever you want to call it. There are plenty of nuts on the internet who are, though. Put that crap on the web where it belongs and stop wasting my time." He picked up the camcorder and shoved it at Jenny.

Jenny took it with a huff. "Told you this would happen," she grumbled to Stacey.

The latter sighed, worry crinkling her expression. "I had to try... God, I hope the thing decides to stay away from people."

Jenny heard the officer snort as she turned to leave. He probably thought Stacey's very real worries were another part of some prank. Anger churned in her gut, and she wished she could pop the tape out of her camcorder and throw it in the man's face. She understood him questioning her motives, but how dare he treat Stacey like that?

As they made their way back to Stacey's SUV in the small parking lot, the memory of the creature's stare burrowed through her head. It must have had some kind of psychic power... maybe, in addition to reading her, it had also planted ideas in her head. What if that was the real reason why she'd been so hesitant to go to the police: because the thing didn't want that kind of attention? It was entirely possible; she had no idea what it was capable of, after all. Last time, she'd sensed its presence too, and then she'd decided not to post her footage on the internet. What if that had been the creature's suggestion as well, and not her rational side warning her she'd look like a nut?

Well, I already made myself look like a nut to the cops. Might as well give the internet a shot. She climbed into the passenger seat of Stacey's car. "You know, at school, they always teach you to listen to cops. That cop said, 'Put that crap on the internet,' and I'm going to do exactly that."

Stacey slid behind the wheel and slammed the car door shut. "Changed your mind?"

"Sure. Can't look like any more of an idiot than I did in there." Jenny nodded at the police station.

"Well, at least if it's out there, people in town might see it. Maybe some will believe it. I kind of wonder if we should go to the *Town Topics* and see if they'll print something, but I know they'd respond the same way the officer did." Stacey pursed her lips as she twisted her key, causing the SUV's engine to growl.

"You're really worried that it'll attack someone on the towpath, aren't you?"

"Yes, I am! And you should be too—you're the one who nearly got eaten!"

"You think it wanted to eat me?" Jenny couldn't help a slight smile.

"I don't know!" With a look of frustration, Stacey backed out of the parking space.

Jenny thought for a moment. "You're right... I should be more scared about what the creature will do. God knows I was plenty scared in the woods. But at the same time... I don't know. I just don't think it wants attention enough to attack anyone in the open."

"So, it'll just attack the next person who wanders off the path like we did? Great."

Jenny wondered if she should be freaking out as much as Stacey was. Though the other girl's demeanor seemed relatively calm, if frustrated, Jenny knew her friend well enough that this was Stacey's version of panic. And maybe Jenny herself was actually calm because she knew that. She'd always found herself having that kind of opposite reaction to others' fear—being scared when others thought there was nothing to worry about, refusing to worry when others were frightened. *Maybe it's a survival instinct. Can't have the whole pack panicking at the same time.*

"Let's go to my place," she said. "We'll splice the footage from the two sightings, take a few stills, and post them on every forum we can get access to. That should get the word out."

"Sounds good." Taking a deep breath, Stacey steered her car onto the road.

Under cover of blackness, the creature remained as still as a stone. Footsteps crunched the forest floor nearby. He remained motionless, silent, virtually invisible. Yet even a shadow could not vanish entirely, and he was prepared to move if the light caught him before the human was within striking range.

Beams flashed across branches, growing brighter and brighter. A low, pulsing hum caused the ground to vibrate. Yet, the creature didn't react.

Something suddenly flew through the branches. The creature's instincts took over, and powerful forelegs struck out.

CHAPTER SIX

The old desktop Jenny's dad had handed down to her was slower than the traffic on Nassau Street, and so she'd opted to plug her comparatively newer laptop into her desktop monitor instead. Maybe seeing what she'd captured on its bigger screen would help her make out... *something*. Though after her failure the last time she'd tried to enhance the picture, she didn't hold much hope.

The monitor flickered to life as it detected the signal from the laptop, onto which she'd uploaded the latest footage from the woods. She got up from her desk chair and turned to Stacey, who'd been watching over her shoulder. "Do you want to give it a try? It didn't go so well for me last time."

"Sure." Stacey took a seat. "I think we don't have the right program for it, but I'll give it a shot."

If that desktop, which still ran Windows 95, hadn't been so slow, they could have divided and conquered as they did before. But even if Jenny had access to another computer, she doubted she would have found anything useful if she tried researching the possibility that the mantis was actually a gray alien. Yet, she couldn't entirely dismiss the notion either. Stacey had been right about the evidence of technology seeming to indicate the extraterrestrial rather than the supernatural. Jenny had certainly never heard of Mothman using a mobile phone or anything. That conjured a rather hilarious image in her head.

As Stacey opened an editing program, Jenny walked over to the terrarium on the bottom shelf of her bookcase. Her pet tarantula presently sat on one of the plastic rocks, relaxing under the heat lamp. "Hey, Mulder. Want to come comfort your mommy? She's had a rough day."

On the other side of the room, Stacey let out a slight laugh. "I'll never get why you got yourself a giant fuzzy spider instead of, like, a ferret or some other normal pet."

"Who wants to be normal? Right, Mulder?" Jenny took off the terrarium's lid, reached inside, and offered the tarantula her hand. Mulder lethargically crawled into her palm, and she lifted him out and petted him with her finger.

Stacey glanced away from the computer screen to throw Jenny a bemused look. "I always knew you were weird, and I'm not exactly Miss On-Trend either, but even for me... this is *weird*. It'd be one thing if you kept Mulder in his box and looked at him now and then, but you treat it like it's a bunny or something, and that's kind of disturbing."

Jenny let out an exaggerated gasp. "How dare you?" She looked down at her pet. "She didn't mean that, baby. Your Aunt Stacey just needs to spend more time with you, that's all."

"No to everything about that sentence." Stacey went back to clicking through the editing software's options.

For the next several minutes, Stacey worked on the footage while Jenny tried to distract herself from what had happened earlier by playing with Mulder. She let him crawl from palm to palm, walk across her leg, tiptoe across her books, sit on her shoulder...

"This software is useless." Stacey backed away from the computer and threw up her hands. "This was the best I could do."

Jenny put Mulder back in his tank and went over to see. A still of the mantis filled the screen, zoomed in so that its head filled nearly the whole thing. Grainy would have been a generous way to describe the quality — that image was more like a mosaic, and not a particularly fine one either.

But whatever Stacey had done, it *did* bring out a few details compared to the near-silhouette Jenny had seen before. The triangular head seemed more pronounced against the background, the bulging eyes more distinct. What hadn't been visible before were two thin antennae sticking out of its forehead. She had to admit, other than those, it *did* look a bit like the drawings of gray aliens she'd seen on TV. But its face was pointier, and she couldn't discern a nose or mouth.

"What do you think?" Stacey asked. "Bug or alien?"

"No idea." Jenny leaned forward, bracing her hand against the back of the chair. "This is really good, though. Did you get any other details?"

"Not really." Stacey dragged the view across the screen, panning down the rest of where the creature would have been standing. All that showed up were brownish blurs; it was impossible to distinguish what was a plant and what was part of the mantis-alien-creature-thing. She zoomed out to show the whole image again, and it became clear that she'd only been able to get details of the creature's head because it happened to move into a space where the sky was visible between the trees, giving it a contrasting background.

Still, it was better than what Jenny had been able to achieve before. A thought occurred to her; there was something she had to see. "Can I take a look?"

"Yeah, sure."

Jenny hit *play* on the newly brightened footage. The wind blew, obscuring the creature, and by the time the branches settled, it had vanished. The sounds of her own breaths and footsteps emitted from the laptop's speakers as she moved toward the spot where the creature had been.

And then came the part she'd been waiting for: the shadowed figure lunging at her. The sound of her scream ripped from the machine, tinny and fuzzy; clearly, she'd blown out the microphone.

She hit *pause*.

"Holy crap!" Stacey's jaw dropped. "You didn't tell me it actually attacked you!"

"That's the thing I wanted to see... because I don't think it did." Jenny narrowed her eyes at the image. All she could make out was a big, useless blur. "I thought it did, but now that I've had some time to think about it, I don't think I could have escaped if it had really wanted me. I'm not exactly a varsity athlete."

Stacey lifted the corner of her mouth. "Well, if nothing else came out of this, at least you have some footage you can use for your movie. You might even give the Blair Witch Project a run for its money."

"I know you're kidding, but once I get over being freaked out, I might be able to use some of this chase footage. I mean, you can't see me in most of it, and if I cut it together with the reaction shot of you falling..." Jenny shook her head. "C'mon, focus! Okay, I wanted to see what jumped out at me..." She rewound the footage in slow motion. The shadowy figure retreated, then vanished from the frame. Unsure what exactly she'd seen, Jenny played it back again, also in slow motion.

Then, she hit *pause* again and rubbed her chin. "Huh. Do you see what I see?"

Stacey leaned closer to the screen. "Yeah, I think I do... That shadow isn't shaped like a mantis."

Only a fragment of whatever had jumped out was visible in the frame, and it was still blurry with motion, but it looked like something with an outreached, humanlike arm attached to a thick torso. That was all that was visible — no head or legs or anything. And the hand was too motion-blurred for Jenny to tell if it actually was a hand. But one thing was for sure: it was not the foreleg of a praying mantis.

"Alien, then?" Stacey said. "Maybe we'd see long fingers if the image weren't so blurred?"

"Or what about... human?"

"Now you think it's a mantis-human hybrid?"

"Of course not! I mean that" — Jenny gestured at the image of the arm — "belongs to a human. Maybe they were the reason the mantis vanished in the first place... maybe they were looking for it like we were."

"Then why did they lunge at you?"

Jenny shrugged. "Maybe all they saw was a shape in the woods and thought I might be the creature?"

"So, you think someone else saw the creature, went looking for it, and decided to tackle it like a football player?"

"I don't know!" Jenny leaned her elbows against her desk. The Solar system stickers she stuck to its brown surface twinkled under the yellow flower-shaped lights in the middle of her ceiling. "Nothing makes any sense!"

Stacey put a hand on her shoulder. "We're tired. Maybe we'll have some better ideas in the morning."

Jenny glanced at her watch. "It's not getting near midnight yet, is it?"

"No, it's only nine, but today has been... a lot. And I have a math quiz that I haven't studied for."

"Okay, I'll talk to you tomorrow, then. I'll have posted the video by then. Maybe someone will have responded. I'll call you if I get anything good."

"Actually, please don't." Stacey gave a sheepish look. "I really do need to study."

"All right." Jenny stood to walk Stacey out, but the latter shook her head.

"You don't have to do that. I know how eager you are to get to posting."

Jenny smiled. "Thanks."

As Stacey left, closing the door behind her, Jenny clicked through some more of the footage. She hoped to catch a glimpse of someone chasing her or more details from the strange floating lights. But even with Stacey's handiwork, she couldn't find anything more than what she'd seen before. *Or maybe it's there, and I'm not observant enough to see it.*

Deciding she could use a break from staring at grainy images of shadows, Jenny set about cutting together the two shots of the creature instead. When she finished, she exported her video into a Windows Media Player format, then opened Firefox and went to Yahoo to search for forums on the paranormal. Uncertain of what she was doing, she clicked on the first one she found that allowed video uploads, ignoring the very inappropriate pop-ups and sidebar ads, and created a new account, using the spare email address she had for this kind of thing. Since she couldn't come up with a clever username and definitely didn't want to use her real one, she just called herself *Moviemaker12345.*

Then, she started a new thread with the subject: *Unexplained creature spotted near Princeton, NJ.* She typed up a quick summary of her experience. After reading over what she'd written, just to make sure she didn't sound like a complete nutjob, she uploaded her video.

Anticipation tingled up her spine as an icon with an upload bar appeared with the words: *In progress...*

The letters blinked in white typewriter-like font, flickering against the black backdrop. *What's taking so long? Is our internet down? Or maybe the site can't handle it?*

The two shots of the creature were so quick, her video was barely five seconds long, so it shouldn't have been too large a file. Perhaps the site was just glitchy. It didn't exactly look like it had been built by professionals.

After what felt like an eternity, a red message appeared on the screen: *Upload failed.*

Annoyed, she decided to give it another go but got the same results.

She tapped her fingers against her desk. Dealing with videos on the internet was always a pain. Maybe it would be better to upload a still for now.

She went back to the video-editing program, clicked until she brought up Stacey's enhanced version, and captured a screenshot close-up of the mantis's face.

She went back to the forum and tried again.

Upload failed. Even though it had been just an image this time, and not a particularly high-res one.

Weird... maybe this website's busted. Jenny went back to the search results and clicked until she found another site that allowed video uploads.

Once again, it didn't work. Once again, she tried with the still instead but didn't get any further.

She went back to the earlier search results, figuring she'd give up on the video and only try to use the still image, and went through each one in turn.

None allowed her to post.

After the sixth try, she stood from her chair and paced across her bedroom. *One bad site's normal. Two's annoying. But... six? Something's wrong...*

She stopped and stared at the computer screen. The problem couldn't be the internet since she'd been able to create the accounts just fine. Only after she typed out her messages and tried to upload an image did they fail on her.

It's almost like someone's purposely keeping me from posting... but that's not possible, is it?

She gripped her arms, suddenly cold. The idea that someone traced her online movements and hacked either the sites or her computer to prevent her from posting almost frightened her more than the creature had. At least she could leave that behind in the woods. But the internet was on her computer, and her computer was in her bedroom...

Spurred by a sudden burst of fear, she rushed to shut down the laptop. She even went as far as to unplug both it and the desktop.

Whether any of that did anything, she didn't know. But one thing seemed certain to her: Someone else out there knew what she'd seen, and they didn't want her telling.

The shadow stalked toward the water. The surrounding blackness made it safer to move, but he was not as much a creature of the night as he needed to be. He navigated around dark shapes, movements slow and deliberate enough that any sound would have been no different than the rustle of a squirrel to any who might have heard.

A light bobbed across the forest. The creature stilled and reached out with his senses.

A human female was approaching at a run, but though she drew closer, she was only following the path and not deliberately heading in the creature's direction. And this human was not the one the creature had sought before.

So, the creature remained still. Had the human but turned, the light from her headlamp would have spilled across the entirety of the creature, robbing him of his shield of shadows.

CHAPTER SEVEN

Jenny stumbled across the forest floor, slipping and tripping on the leaves and roots and rocks. A fluttering noise sounded behind her, and she whirled.

The creature stood directly ahead, only its triangular face and enormous, bulbous black eyes visible – a floating head amid the shadows.

Jenny tried to scream, but no sound came out. The creature held her stare, its eyes glinting and boring into hers, reading her. She backed away, but it didn't pursue. Her heel caught on something, and she landed hard on the ground.

It remained still, watching.

Jenny picked herself up. A calm feeling rolled over her like a gentle wave upon the beach. The creature remained motionless except for a slight quirk of its head.

She reached toward it…

Something crashed through the shrubs nearby. The creature retreated, vanishing into the shadows.

A figure lunged at her –

Jenny woke up with a gasp, her heart pounding. She blinked several times, taking in the silvery parallel stripes on her ceiling made by the moonlight spilling through her blinds and reminding herself that the chase was over, that she was in her bedroom, and that the creature was nowhere nearby.

She rolled over, pulling her comforter over her head. Stacey would kill her, but Jenny knew she couldn't leave this alone—not yet.

"I can't believe I let you drag me out here *again*," Stacey grumbled as she stepped between two bushes. "You know what Einstein said about the definition of insanity, right?"

"Hey, I just asked you for a ride." Holding her camcorder in one hand, Jenny gripped a tree truck for support as she jumped over a large rock. She'd need to buy a new set of tapes soon with all the footage she'd been capturing lately. "You can go if you want."

"I'm not leaving you out here alone. Not after last time." Stacey shuddered. "But this time, we're leaving well before sundown, no matter what you say. I'm not about to be caught out here at night again."

"Me neither." Jenny gave her a smile. "I'm glad you're here, by the way. Thanks for coming along on my stupid adventure."

"Only because I don't want to hear about your dead body on the news if something attacks you again. I mean it, Jenny. We're going at six. I'll drag you back if I have to."

Jenny tried to recognize anything familiar or distinctive from the last time she'd been out in the woods. Though she wasn't sure what she hoped to find by returning to the spot where she last saw the creature, it was a start. She'd re-watched the footage from her camera enough times that she was pretty sure she'd know the particular configuration of trees and bushes if she saw them.

A featureless gray sky stretched above this time, dimming what should have been the brightest time of day. But since it was finally the weekend again, at least she hadn't had to wait until after school to resume her search.

Stacey, who'd brought her camcorder as well, panned the device across the woods. Her other hand remained tightly clenched around a little canister of pepper spray she'd insisted on bringing. "I don't know what more you're hoping to find. You already got the creature on video twice, and that hasn't led to anything."

"Third time's the charm?" Jenny gave the pepper spray a slantwise look. "Do you really think that'll be enough to fend off the creature?"

"It's better than nothing, okay? I couldn't exactly get a Taser on short notice. Anyway, you still haven't answered my question. When is enough, enough?"

"I just know there's more out here." Jenny dragged her gaze across the ground, though she wasn't sure what she was searching for. A piece of tech that fell off whatever had caused those strange noises and lights, maybe? A distinctive imprint in the ground? "Something profoundly weird is going on. If I'd been able to post my video—or even just the still—I might have left it at that for a spell. But someone actively stopped me from posting... who does that?"

"Curses upon whoever it was, because if they hadn't interfered, we'd be working on my movie right now instead of chasing shadows."

"Hey, I already promised I'd work on it with you after school on Monday!"

"Even if we haven't found anything more about the creature by then?"

"Even if. But admit it: You want to know what this thing is as much as I do. Especially since it could be a danger to everyone who uses the towpath, remember?"

Stacey sighed. "It really doesn't feel right leaving it out there without anyone else knowing, but I just don't know—" She broke off. "Did you hear that?"

"What?" The snap of twigs filled the air, and Jenny jumped. She whirled in the direction of the noise, camcorder up, and held her breath. Stacey remained just as still beside her.

The forest floor crunched steadily. Those were footsteps—they had to be. Jenny watched keenly, wondering if this would be the moment the creature revealed itself again. Yet something was missing... that uncanny feeling that had accompanied both previous encounters was absent. And the steps didn't sound right for a six-legged insect, though she'd never seen its lower half. For all she knew, it walked like a human. A shiver of anticipation ran down her spine as the footsteps grew closer, closer...

A hand pushed back a leafy branch—a very human-looking hand with pale skin and thick knuckles. Soon a face followed as a man poked his head between the bushes and stepped forward. An unkempt brown beard framed his face, and he wore loose jeans and a baggy black sweatshirt. The large gray pack he carried on his shoulder could have held both Jenny and Stacey's bags and all their contents inside; it looked like the kind hikers carried to go camping. He looked to be in his mid-twenties. A baseball cap shaded the top half of his face.

"Hey! What do you think you're doing, filming me?" he demanded.

Stacey yelped and held up her pepper spray.

He held up his hands. "Whoa! Put that down!"

Stacey lowered the canister slowly.

Jenny pressed the button on her camcorder to stop recording. "Sorry, I didn't know who was approaching. Thought you might be... something else."

The man, who was about half a head taller than Jenny and had a heavyset frame, gave her a stern look. "You girls shouldn't be out here. It isn't safe. What are you doing anyway?"

"School project." Jenny took note of the large backpack he carried and the thick black gloves he wore. "What about you?"

"I'm a researcher. But I've received survival training and worked with park rangers before. I'll bet you can't say the same."

"Survival training? Park rangers?" Jenny let out a snort. "Have you forgotten we're in *Princeton*?"

"All the same, you girls should go back to the path before something bad happens, and no one's around to help. Even if you've got cell phones to call someone, how would they ever find you? Do you even know where you are? Your GPS coordinates? Your proximity to the nearest road or marked path?"

"Pfft, of course," Jenny replied, even as her mind muttered, *Nope.*

The man pointed at Stacey's camcorder. "You're not recording, are you?"

"I turned it off." Nervousness colored Stacey's tone.

"Why are you so squirrelly about being recorded anyway?" Jenny asked. "Got something to hide?"

"I just don't want my face on some stranger's camera." The man crossed his arms. "If I were caught filming you without your permission, I'd get arrested and labeled a pervert. Now, society doesn't see things the same way the other way around, but that doesn't mean it's okay for you to do."

"Fine." Jenny shoved her camcorder into her backpack and held up her empty hands. "Happy?"

"Towpath's that way." The man pointed behind him. "Keep going straight, and don't get turned around. Go on, then."

"We don't have to—"

"Forget it, Jenny." Stacey grabbed Jenny's arm and gave her a meaningful look. "Let's go."

Deciding it was pointless to stand around arguing with a stranger, Jenny went with her friend. "What was that all about?" she asked, keeping her voice low.

Stacey shrugged. "I'm guessing he's doing field research or something for the university, maybe in the environmental engineering department, and doesn't want two high schoolers distracting him from his work."

Jenny looked over her shoulder. The man was still within eyeshot. He'd taken off his backpack and was rummaging through it. "Or maybe he's out here for the same reason we are. Maybe he *was* doing field research and stumbled upon the mantis like we did. I should go back and ask—"

She didn't finish her sentence. A chill frosted her skin, and that uncanny feeling washed over her, telling her that the creature was nearby. She stood frozen for a moment, then hurried to dig her camcorder out of her backpack.

"What is it?" Stacey asked.

"It's here," Jenny whispered. She glanced back toward the man, but he'd vanished from sight.

Stacey's gaze darted through the trees. "I don't see anything." Her voice was barely audible.

Jenny turned on her camcorder and took a step forward. The strange feeling seemed to tug her back as if saying she was going the wrong way. She spun and stepped in the opposite direction. This time, the feeling grew stronger. *Must be getting warmer...*

Stacey gripped her shoulder. "Where are you going?"

"It's that way... I know it. I think it's calling to me." She tried to continue, but Stacey held her back.

"I don't think this is a good idea, Jenny. You have no idea what it wants with you. For all you know, it's doing that thing we learned about in biology where predators lure their prey into an ambush."

It suddenly hit Jenny how right Stacey was and how foolish it had been for her to try following the silent call to where the creature waited. She'd aced her paper on the *Odyssey* after all; she knew how sirens worked.

Jenny shook her head rapidly, as if she could fling the uncanny feeling—and possibly the creature's psychic calls—out of her skull. "I say we approach, but go carefully. It didn't attack before, and this could be our best chance at learning more."

"I'm still not sure the shadow on your camera wasn't the creature somehow."

"Well, I am."

"Jenny..."

Jenny shook off Stacey's hand and took a slow step in the direction the psychic call seemed to be coming from. Stacey didn't try to stop her this time but held out the pepper spray as if it were a gun and she was a cop on *Law and Order* about to kick down a suspect's door.

Part of Jenny wished she'd thought to bring something similar. *But I won't need it, right? You don't want to hurt us… right?*

The feeling grew stronger. It watched, waited, just out of sight. Or maybe it was already within sight, and Jenny's eyes weren't discerning enough to make out its camouflaged body amid the mess of plants.

She was so busy looking that she didn't watch her steps, and her foot caught on a protruding root. She tripped with a gasp. Her face smashed into the dirt, and the camcorder went tumbling.

"Are you okay?" Stacey rushed up to her, crouching down to help her up.

Jenny had barely made it onto her knees when she fell backward in shock.

The creature stood over her—its mantis-like shape unmistakable from this close, from its claw-like forelegs to its thin antennae to the four translucent brown wings outstretched behind it.

CHAPTER EIGHT

Stacey's jaw dropped, but Jenny clapped a hand over her friend's mouth before the scream had a chance to escape. Some instinct had driven her to do it, a strong impression the sound would only draw unwanted attention. The man they'd encountered a moment ago couldn't be too far off, and whoever he was, Jenny didn't want him interfering.

She stared up at the creature, which towered over the two crouched girls. Even though its outstretched wings and raised forelegs seemed menacing, Jenny got the distinct sense that it didn't mean her any harm. That uncanny feeling churned through her, and she knew the creature had to be trying to communicate with her again.

What do you want? Her breathing felt painfully loud as she remained where she knelt, torn between fear and fascination.

Beside her, Stacey lifted the pepper spray, but Jenny shook her head. So far, the creature seemed content to remain where it stood, but who knew what it would do if attacked?

"Well, it's not a gray alien," Jenny said with a dry smile.

Stacey, apparently stunned to speechlessness, gave Jenny an incredulous look.

Jenny stood slowly, her gaze pinned on the mantis. It lowered its wings, which made a soft *whooshing* sound as they folded behind. She took in as many details as she could — the mottled brown-and-black coloring, the snakeskin-like texture of its exterior, the sharp spikes along the inner edges of its sharply bent forelegs. Then, she noticed that one of its four spindly hind legs had a piece of thick metal wrapped around it.

What is that? she wondered.

As if in reply, the mantis stepped toward her. Jenny gasped while Stacey jumped up and scrambled backward. But then the mantis stopped, and Jenny realized the metal-wrapped leg remained where it was.

"Stacey, look." Jenny pointed. "I think it's trapped."

"Good." With shaking hands, Stacey reached for her backpack. "That means it can't reach us. Now, I'll get a video, and then let's get out of here."

"But who could have done it?" Jenny tried to make out the details of the trap but couldn't discern anything from the metal. "You know this means others are hunting for it, right? I'll bet that's what the guy who called himself a researcher was actually doing out here."

"Well, if this is his trap, he'll be back soon enough."

"Maybe." Jenny stared into those enormous, featureless eyes. *What are you? Can you hear my thoughts?*

An image flashed through Jenny's head: her own face staring back at her as it would look to someone a yard taller. Except it wasn't a mirror image—it was slightly distorted, with all color leeched out. Yet she could perceive every infinitesimal movement of her body, from the smallest wisps of hair shifting by her face to the slight pulse from the veins in her neck to the tremor in her fingers so subtle, she couldn't feel it herself.

She blinked in surprise. In her mind, the image blinked as well. She furrowed her brow—as did the image, except it showed a lot more crinkles than what Jenny was accustomed to seeing in her reflection. A realization occurred to her, and she experimentally flexed the fingers of one hand. The image followed suit. *It's showing me what I look like from its point of view...*

The image vanished. Jenny tilted her head, wondering what that had meant.

Then, another image filled her head: She saw herself leaning down to pick up the camcorder, which presently lay right below one of the mantis's forelegs. In the vision, the mantis didn't move as she picked up the device.

That image faded too, and the mantis lowered its head toward where the camcorder lay.

You want me to retrieve it... you're telling me you're going to let me. Jenny reached forward slowly.

"Jenny..." Stacey gripped her shoulder.

Jenny glanced at her. "It's all right." She looked up at the mantis. *You're not going to hurt me, are you?*

The previous image filled her head again—her picking up the camcorder without interference.

Jenny gave Stacey as confident a smile as she could muster. "Don't worry. I'm just going to get my camcorder."

Stacey pulled the pepper spray from her pocket and held it up.

"Don't!" Jenny grabbed her friend's arm and looked up at the mantis in alarm.

The mantis didn't react, but another image filled Jenny's head. It was the same one as before—of Jenny picking up the camcorder—but this time, Stacey was in it too, holding the pepper spray up at the mantis, which remained unmoving.

Jenny wasn't sure how to react. Neither was Stacey, it seemed, since her arm remained where Jenny had shoved it, midway between her pocket and an outstretched posture.

The image replayed in Jenny's head. *You're telling me it's okay... that you'll let Stacey threaten you if that means I might trust you. Is that right?*

The version of the vision with Stacey holding the pepper spray replayed for a third time.

"Jenny, what's happening?" Stacey's voice trembled.

"It's communicating with me psychically, putting images in my head. I think it wants us to trust it. Did it say anything to you?"

"No... Jenny, I don't mean to sound like I'm accusing you of anything, but... are you sure you're sensing what you think you are?"

"Positive." That was probably the first truly certain thought Jenny had had in a week. She glanced at Stacey. "Do you sense anything?"

"No... I'm not sure what you're talking about."

Jenny looked up at the mantis. *Why can't she hear you too?*

Another image filled Jenny's head: of both Jenny and Stacey standing side-by-side. Stacey's image vanished, and Jenny's grew larger.

You're saying you only want to communicate with me?

The image repeated.

I'll take that as a yes.

As if to confirm, the image repeated for a third time. Then, another replay of Jenny retrieving the camcorder while Stacey held her pepper spray.

Though it apparently couldn't talk, the mantis couldn't have made itself clearer.

All right, let's do it, then.

Jenny released Stacey's arm. "Go ahead and hold up your pepper spray if it makes you feel better. I'm getting my camcorder."

Stacey raised the small canister. "This is a terrible idea…"

Jenny kept her gaze on the creature as she crouched down to pick up the camcorder. As it had in the visions, the mantis remained perfectly still.

Jenny snatched up the device and rushed backward several steps. The mantis remained motionless, watching. She turned on the camcorder. The mantis didn't move as she zoomed in and panned the lens up and down, making sure to capture as much detail as she could.

"Do you have enough now?" Stacey, still holding up the pepper spray, took a step backward. "Can we get out of here and call the cops? That video must be enough to convince them this time."

"I…"

Jenny trailed off as another image filled her head. This time, it showed the mantis slowly reaching one foreleg toward her—and her reaching out a hand to meet it.

What are you trying to tell me?

What happened next reminded Jenny of a movie flashback montage in her head, except all the images were filtered through that colorless-yet-detailed view, and a jumble of sensations accompanied them.

First, it showed the forest floor from what had to be the mantis's point of view, judging by the forelegs that kept popping in and out of view. A feeling of urgency accompanied it. Then, it showed Jenny setting up her camcorder in the distance, with Stacey standing on her mark, wearing the costume dress for Jenny's movie. A feeling of fear descended, and the mantis froze in place, blending into the background. Then a sensation that could only be described as hope, though she wasn't sure if she'd interpreted it correctly. Next came more forest-floor images and a yearning sensation. That one felt almost familiar, since it was just like the way Jenny had felt when she combed through the woods for an answer. And then Jenny appeared again, closer this time.

You were looking for me. Jenny's eyes widened. *You happened upon us when we were making my movie, and you homed in on me for some reason. And then, the whole time I was looking for you, you were seeking me too.*

The image of herself from the mantis's point of view filled her head again, and the feeling of urgency repeated.

Were you the one that jumped out at me the other night?

The image of herself shifted — the setting was darker, and she was standing in a different position. She took a step closer — and then a humanlike silhouette jumped out from behind a tree. The view changed to that of trees whisking by. It reminded Jenny of what she'd seen while fleeing.

You're telling me that it was a human who did that, and you ran away too.

Jenny was relieved to know that she'd been right about what had attacked her, but that only led her to wonder who that human could have been.

What do you want from me?

The mantis bent its head toward the metal ring around its leg.

Another jumble of images and sensations filled Jenny's mind, but this time even more disjointed. She saw metal bars and flashing lights, heard unintelligible mutterings and deep whirring noises. They reminded her of the ones she'd encountered the previous night, albeit louder and harsher, and she wondered if that was how they sounded to the mantis. Feelings of urgency and fight-or-flight panic swirled through her, growing more and more powerful until Jenny's heart thundered from secondhand anxiety.

She breathed hard in an effort not to let the fear overwhelm her.

"Jenny?" Stacey's voice was soft, uncertain.

"I'm all right," Jenny managed.

Loudly rumbling machinery, brilliant swaths of lights, sharp metal things whose shapes were impossible to pinpoint through the sensory overload...

Then, the quiet of the woods. A moment of calm, of belonging. Those powerful forelegs snatching a fish from the canal, a feeling of nourishment that came after a hearty meal.

You escaped something terrible. What happened?

Instead of an answer, the image of Jenny reaching toward the mantis's foreleg reappeared.

You want my help, don't you? But why me?

Mulder the Tarantula flashed through Jenny's mind, sitting in Jenny's palm, the forefinger of her other hand gently petting his fuzzy back. A feeling of warmth filled her, though she wasn't sure if that came from the mantis or if it was just her fondness for her pet.

Her lips curved subconsciously. *You read my mind and learned I like giant bugs.*

Several more images flashed, depicting various joggers, dog walkers, and passersby in the distance—including Stacey. With all of them came a feeling of trepidation and uncertainty.

You were looking for help for a while but didn't know who to trust until you found the girl with a creepy pet. Jenny felt weirdly honored to have been chosen that way. *I don't understand, though. You're so big, and you have wings. What do you need me for?*

An image of the mantis standing still but for its rapidly fluttering wings appeared. Jenny could almost feel the strain in her own body as the creature struggled to get off the ground but failed. She nodded with understanding.

Your wings can't carry you... something went wrong with whatever happened to you before, which you don't understand either.

"Jenny..." Stacey tapped Jenny's shoulder. "What's going on?"

"It was telling me why it called to me." Jenny relaxed slightly. Even though she'd somehow known that the mantis posed no threat to her, now the last shades of doubt fell away. "Something awful happened to it, something involving technology, though I couldn't make out what. It escaped, but it needs help, and it psychically read a lot of humans before it picked me... because of Mulder."

"Because you love something that most find horrifying." Stacey put the pepper spray back in her pocket. "Well, I guess if it wanted to attack, we'd both be dead by now."

"It's scared, Stacey. It doesn't want to attack anyone... it eats fish, not people. I think it just wants to be left alone, but something's after it, and that's why it needs a human's help." Jenny took a few tentative steps toward the mantis's trapped leg. "I have to get that thing off of it."

"Are you sure that's a good idea?" Stacey looked as if she was going to continue but abruptly whirled to look back.

The mantis shifted in place, and Jenny sensed its agitation. "What's going on?" she asked.

"Someone's coming," Stacey said, and at the same time, an image filled Jenny's head showing several figures approaching, indistinct other than their human-shaped silhouettes, but undeniable in their movements.

A low whirring noise reverberated across the forest—the same one from the night before.

"I'd better hurry." Jenny rushed forward.

She barely heard the *whooshing* noise before something flew over her head.

A sensation of panic filled her, and the mantis thrashed. Jenny jumped out of the way before one of its flailing forelegs and floundering wings could strike her. Something glinted against its long neck: what looked like a metal dart.

"Got it!" a man's voice called out.

The nearby brush parted, and two pale hands gripping some kind of gun poked out.

"No!" Jenny cried.

A second dart embedded itself in the mantis's neck beside the first, and the creature fell to the ground with a great *thud*.

CHAPTER NINE

Jenny stared in horror at the fallen creature. The psychic sensations vanished from her mind, which suddenly felt empty. No more uncanny feeling rumbling in her gut, no more rudimentary emotions that weren't hers. She hadn't realized how connected she must have been with the mantis until that connection broke.

The deep whirring noise continued, seeming to make her blood vibrate in her veins.

A man shoved his way through the brush, carrying what appeared to be a thin black-and-brown rifle. Tall and lanky with a shock of thick blond hair and a five-o-clock shadow, he stomped forward with the swagger of a hunter that had brought down a prized predator. But he wasn't dressed in camo or anything; he wore the same baggy jeans as seemingly every guy in town, and his too-large t-shirt, featuring a wolf mascot, looked like it had been caught from a cannon at a football game.

"What did you do?" Jenny cried.

The man narrowed his harsh brown eyes at her. "Who the hell are you?"

"Who the hell are *you?*"

"Hey!" A woman in a denim jacket with a black topknot appeared from between two bushes. A large pack sat on her shoulders. "What's going on? Who're these kids?"

"That's what I want to know." The man glanced between Jenny and Stacey with a scowl.

Jenny kept her camcorder up, but Stacey, apparently frozen in fear, clutched her backpack to her chest. Jenny wasn't sure when the other girl had taken it off. *C'mon, Stacey! Where's that pepper spray when it could do us some good?*

"They're just high-school kids." A third person joined the scene: the same bearded man in a baseball cap that had encountered Jenny and Stacey earlier. "They won't be a problem. Right, girls?"

Jenny scowled. "What's going on here?"

"Nothing that has anything to do with you." The man in the baseball cap shrugged the giant pack off his shoulders and lowered it slowly to the ground.

"This is private business," the blond man said. "I suggest you leave."

"What kind of business is *this*?" Infuriated, Jenny thrust her hand downward, and an unexpected surge of tears made her eyes burn. "It wasn't hurting you! What did you do to it?"

"Calm down. It's only a tranquilizer gun." The man in the baseball cap nodded toward the other man's weapon.

The mantis's foreleg twitched, and the man aimed again.

"No!" Jenny jumped in front of him.

"Jenny!" Stacey cried.

The woman leaped at the blond man and seized his arm, causing the shot to miss widely. "What do you think you're doing? You can't shoot a kid, not unless you want every cop from here to Trenton coming after us!"

"She stepped in front of *me*!" the man protested.

"Give me that." The woman snatched the weapon away. "A double dose is more than enough to keep the specimen knocked out while we transfer it. Overdo it and you could kill the thing. What good would that do us?"

"What's all the fuss?" A barrel-chested man with a shaved head approached, followed closely by a muscular woman with a brown braid. Both held slim weapons identical to the blond man's tranquilizer gun. "Got your message."

"Can you turn that thing off?" The woman with the brown braid gave the man in the baseball cap a sharp look. "Clearly, we've found the thing, and it's giving me a headache."

"Oh, right." The man with the baseball cap crouched beside his pack, unzipped the top, and reached inside. A clicking noise ensued, and then the sound vanished.

So that's what the noise was. Jenny turned her camcorder toward the pack and craned her neck, trying to get a better look. *Not aliens, after all. Too bad.*

"What is that?" she asked.

The man with the baseball cap ignored her.

The bald man looked down at the creature, approaching slowly. "This won't be fun to carry. The others are on their way."

"Others?" Jenny glanced around at the five strangers. "Who are you?"

"None of your business." The blond man took a threatening step toward her. "I told you to get out of here."

Jenny stared up at him defiantly. "No. Stacey, call the cops."

Stacey nodded, and her hand inched toward her backpack, but she kept it clutched to her chest for some reason, even though that meant some awkward maneuvering to reach the small, zippered pocket in the front.

The blond man let out a chuckle. "What are you going to tell them? That you found a giant mantis knocked out in the woods? We'll be long gone by the time they get here—if they even bother to come. I guarantee that no one will believe you."

"Don't be so sure." Jenny held her camera a little higher to make her point.

"You think I didn't notice your little documentary?" The man lunged at her and ripped the device from her hand.

"Hey!" Jenny reached for it, but she was too late—the man smashed the camera against a rock in the ground.

Bits of plastic exploded from the small machine, and the minuscule screen popped out of the side, neon lights flashing across it. The man's heavy boot came down, shattering the lens. The tape spilled out of the side, and he smashed it and ground his heel.

"No!" None of Jenny's efforts to rescue the camcorder did her any good, and she stared in dismay at the destroyed device.

An unexpected sob bubbled up her throat, and she crouched over the plastic fragments, gathering up as many as she could even though she could already tell there was no chance of fixing it. It wasn't just that she'd lost all her footage, including some of her movie for school. That was—that was her *camera*. No, not even hers. Her family's. Mom and Dad would probably buy a new one eventually, but they'd never let her use it after she'd been responsible for breaking the last one.

"Was that really necessary?" the woman with the black topknot muttered to the blond man.

"Like I said, this is private business," the man replied.

"Come on, Jenny." Stacey gripped Jenny's arm and pulled her up. Her backpack now sat awkwardly on one shoulder. "Let's go."

Clutching the broken camera to her chest, Jenny looked around at the five strangers. What was she supposed to do, fight them? She'd certainly never win, especially since three of them had weapons.

"This isn't right, and you know it." She glanced down at the tranquilized mantis. "When I first spotted him, I thought he was a monster, but I was wrong, wasn't I?"

"Spare us the clichés." The blond man rolled his eyes and aimed his tranquilizer gun at her.

"What are you doing?" the man with the shaved head stepped toward him.

"Oh, a little tranquilizer won't hurt them," the man said lightly. "They'll probably only get a little hangover when they wake up... not that they should know what one feels like. That said, I'd hate to waste two perfectly good doses."

"*Jenny!*" Stacey pulled hard at Jenny's arm. "Enough! You know you can't win this, and I don't want to get knocked out!"

"You'd better listen to your friend." The man jerked his head at the woods. "Shoo."

Jenny had much more to say, but none of it would do any good. A helpless sensation descended, and she hated it with every fiber of her being. She wished she could morph into one of the sci-fi action heroines she loved watching so much—Sarah Connor or Wonder Woman or Princess Leia—but she was just... just Jenny.

She reluctantly let Stacey drag her away from the scene by the arm, feeling like the biggest failure to ever walk the earth.

"Hey, you should put that in your backpack." Stacey nodded at the broken camcorder.

"Fine, if you'll give me back my arm," Jenny grumbled, though she felt bad the moment she said it. Stacey wasn't the one she was mad at, after all.

Stacey released her, and Jenny unzipped her backpack and dumped the ruined device inside for all the good it would do her.

"We can reshoot any parts of your movie you lost." Stacey gave her an encouraging smile. "You can borrow my camcorder."

Jenny smiled back. "Thanks." She blew out a breath. "Ugh, sorry for being a drama queen for real this time. It's just..."

"He broke your camera, and you couldn't stop him. You have every right to be upset."

"That, and the mantis... I know you don't get it, but he was counting on me. He sought me out because he thought I could help... he *chose* me, and I failed him." Jenny hung her head. "Now, we'll never know what's going on."

"Maybe... or maybe not." Stacey lowered her voice to a whisper, and her eyes glinted.

"What do you mean?"

"I'll tell you later." She glanced over her shoulder.

Understanding, Jenny didn't press the matter. She tried to see what might be going on back at the scene with the mantis but couldn't make out anything in particular. "Who do you think those people are?" she wondered out loud. "Is this some kind of... I don't know... government experiment, do you think?"

"If it were, they would've flashed badges or something."

"True. And it's not like Area 51's around here."

"It's got to be some kind of private experiment... a corporation or something." Stacey marched forward at a brisk pace.

It took less time than Jenny had expected to find their way back to the towpath.

Once they reached the familiar gravel walkway, Stacey swung her backpack in front of her again. "Okay, I didn't want to say anything where those jerks could have heard us, but now that we're back in a public-ish space, I think we should be okay."

As if to emphasize her point, a pair of cyclists approached, ringing the bells of their sporty red bikes. Jenny stepped out of the way as they rode by. "What's going on?"

Stacey unzipped her backpack and tilted it toward Jenny. "You weren't the only one who brought a camcorder, remember?"

Jenny's eyes widened. She took in the position of the camera — whose lens was right up against the zipper — and the blinking lights indicating that it was still recording. Stacey must not have zipped up her backpack all the way, leaving a peephole for it to keep filming what was going on. No wonder why she'd been clutching her backpack in front of her the whole time.

"You're *amazing!*" Jenny grinned. "Oh, my God, I can't believe... I mean..."

"Hang on, don't get too excited. I don't know if this captured anything useful. For all we know, I didn't position it right, and it only got the inside of my backpack." Stacey's lips twitched. "But it's better than nothing, right?"

"Right!" Jenny drew a deep breath. "Okay, this means we have a chance at proving what happened."

"I don't think that's what we should do. We'll probably be dismissed as pranksters again, even with close-up footage of the mantis. But we might find something that could tell us more about who those people were. Maybe after that, we'll have enough to try the cops again."

"And find out what they've done with that poor creature." Hope sparked in Jenny's heart. "What are we waiting for, then? Let's go home and see what we can find."

CHAPTER TEN

The footage of the mantis was unmistakable this time. Jenny was sure that if they brought what they'd captured on Stacey's camera to the police, the authorities would either have to admit the creature was real or believe two high schoolers were responsible for visual effects so realistic, they'd put Hollywood to shame.

Back in her bedroom, the gray sky dimming outside the window, Jenny leaned against the back of the chair while Stacey clicked through the images her camcorder had captured.

"What do you think?" Stacey asked. "I take back what I said before—maybe we should go to the cops after all. They might not believe the rest of it, but this"—she gestured at the screen—"is pretty persuasive."

"Funny that you say that because I realized I was looking at things wrong before." Jenny faced her terrarium, and her eyes combed over the plastic plants until she found Mulder resting in one corner. "I was so excited at the idea of proving that something incredible had happened that I didn't stop to think about who it was actually happening *to*."

"What do you mean?"

Jenny pursed her lips and made her way over to the terrarium. The images the mantis had psychically shown her flicked through her head like a slideshow. Her with her hand outstretched toward its foreleg. Her picking up the camera while it stood still, allowing Stacey to threaten it with pepper spray in hopes that would be enough to make her trust it. Some might have laughed at the notion of an over-sized insect having such deliberate thoughts and emotions, but Jenny had experienced enough to believe that it was as intelligent as she was, if not more so.

She opened the tank, reached inside, and let her tarantula crawl into her palm. Straightening, she turned to Stacey and held out her pet. "Want to hold him?"

Stacey recoiled. "Ugh, you know my answer's always no."

"Why? You know he won't hurt you."

"I just... don't want to be near it, okay?"

"And you're not alone in that." Jenny stroked the tarantula's back. "Mulder's tiny compared to a human, but if I set him loose in school, few would pick him up and try to find him a home. Most would run and scream or try to stomp on him. And that's for a little pet tarantula. What do you think they'd do to an eight-foot-tall mantis?"

Stacey leaned her elbows against her knees. "What are you getting at?"

"Let's say we go to the cops, and they believe us this time. They'll send people into the woods to hunt down the mantis. True, it's not there anymore—who knows where those strangers took it—but if he ever escaped again, and the cops or whoever they called in actually found him..." Jenny trailed off with a sigh. "We went to them before because we thought it might be dangerous, but now we know that's not true. In fact, *we're* the danger."

Stacey glanced at the screen, which was paused on a close-up of the mantis's face. "You're saying you want to keep this to ourselves."

Jenny nodded.

"What about those people in the woods?"

"I doubt the cops would assign a detective to track down a bully who smashed a camera."

Stacey shot her annoyed look. "Pretty sure what happened counts as assault. You want to go after them, don't you? Figure out who they are, what they're doing to the mantis? It might help if someone else is on our side when we confront the bad guys."

"Even if we could get them to listen, we might lead them right to the mantis."

Stacey twisted her mouth. She started to say something, then paused and blew out a breath. "Fine, I guess this means we're on our own."

"I don't like it either." Jenny returned to the terrarium and let Mulder crawl back inside. "Maybe the smart thing to do would be to forget the whole thing, especially since the mantis isn't out there anymore."

"But the *right* thing to do is to try to find it and help it," Stacey spoke with an exaggerated tone of exasperation. "Spare me the noble speech.

I already know you're not going to quit until the mantis is free, and neither will I. Sure, it creeps me out, and I wasn't the one it chose to psychically talk to, but I've come too far to walk away now. Just promise me one thing."

"What is it?"

"That at some point we'll actually finish our filmmaking projects."

Jenny let out a quick laugh. "Okay."

"Preferably before the deadline, though Mr. Fernando might be nice enough to grant you an extension if you tell him your camera broke."

"I said, okay!"

Stacey grinned. "Great. Now, let's see if we can figure out who those weirdos in the woods were."

She turned back to the monitor and clicked through the footage. Much of it was obscured by her shifting backpack, but it did manage to capture bits and pieces of the scene.

Jenny scowled upon seeing the blond man again on the screen. She wanted to punch him through the LCD display.

Stacey paused on a still of him and zoomed in. The image was too blurry and pixelated to make out any details, so she soon moved on. She paused again on an image of the woman with black hair, and then again on the man with the baseball cap. In none of those instances did they manage to discern anything useful from the low-quality footage.

"There must be something," Jenny muttered. "Say, we know what they look like, and we have these images. Maybe we could try searching the web to find out who they are."

"Where would we start?" Stacey didn't take her eyes off the screen. "It's not like there's a database of people who live in New Jersey, and they could be from out-of-state for all we know."

"True..."

The light faded outside, and Jenny's legs grew tired from standing over the desk, so she left her bedroom to fetch a second chair.

"Jenny!" Mom's voice called up from the first floor of their spacious suburban house—the kind with a three-car garage and a meticulously maintained green lawn. "Is Stacey staying over for dinner, or are you two going to eat out again?"

It's dinnertime already? Jenny glanced at her watch. Somehow, she and Stacey had spent two hours hunting through the footage without any luck. "We'll eat out again!" Jenny didn't have to check with her friend before answering; the answer was always the same. One of the greatest perks of Stacey having a driver's license and a car was that they could indulge their junk food cravings on a whim.

Jenny's mom approached from the staircase, her short black perm, streaked with dark red highlights, forming a cloud-shaped shadow on the cream-colored wall behind her. "You've been spending a lot of time on this film project. Don't forget you have other classes too."

Jenny gave Mom a sheepish look. She still hadn't worked up the courage to tell her about the broken camera. "I haven't."

Lines formed between Mom's penciled black brows. "You look worried. You've been very stressed since you began making this movie for school, more stressed than you were for your midterm exams."

"Making a movie is a lot of work." Jenny shrugged. "And I want mine to be good—"

"Jenny!" Stacey called from the bedroom. "Come see this!"

"Gotta go." Jenny rushed away from Mom, who shook her head and walked back down the stairs.

Jenny practically sprinted through the door and kicked it shut behind her. "Did you find something?"

"I think so!" Stacey pointed at the screen, which was now zoomed in on the bald man's pocket. An orange card with black lettering poked out.

Jenny gasped. "That's a Princeton University ID card! My dad has one just like it! That means this guy is associated somehow. He looked a bit old to be a student—faculty, maybe?"

"Or a grad student?" Stacey rubbed her chin. "I wonder if they're all associated. Maybe the mantis is part of a university project."

"I wouldn't be surprised. Ivy Leagues pride themselves on their mad scientists. And it seemed like they had some really advanced, possibly experimental tech. It would make sense if it was developed in a university lab." Jenny jittered with excitement. "Most—if not all—of the department websites post pictures of their faculty and students. There *is* a database, after all! Well, sort of. I mean, it's not perfect since the sites only show people *in* their departments, and it's possible this guy is a really mature-looking underclassman who hasn't declared yet. But it's better than nothing. And who knows, while we're searching, we might find some of the others too."

"That could take a while." Stacey stood from the chair and stretched. "And I'm getting hungry. I say we get something to eat, and then I'll drop you off back here and go home so I can use my computer to look through websites too. We'll divide and conquer."

"Sounds like a plan. Where do you want to go for dinner?"

"One sec." Stacey sat back down. "I took some stills of the strangers and I want to email them to myself. I'm pretty sure I remember what all of them look like, but it never hurts to have a reference." She opened a browser and navigated to the Hotmail site, which was still logged into Jenny's account.

A few unread messages sat in her inbox, probably all school announcements or junk mail. Jenny started to glance away but did a double-take when she noticed the subject line of the one at the top: *The Mantis.*

"Wait!" she cried before Stacey could log out. "I need to see something. Can you move over?"

Stacey got up, and her eyes widened. She must have glimpsed the same subject line.

The sender was "Anonymous," and it was clear that the email address used was a burner one—several random letters and numbers strung together. Jenny rushed to open the message and read its contents:

> *I know you're looking for the mantis, and I know you tried to upload images of it before but failed. If you want to know what's going on, meet me at the university on Friday. Act like you're visiting the college like all the other kids who are thinking about applying and take the 1 PM campus tour. I'll meet you along the way.*

Jenny reread the message, and a cold sweat broke over her brow. Someone *had* been watching her online. This confirmed it. But who? How? Why?

"Well, there's a twist for you," Stacey said nervously. "What do you think they want with us?"

"No idea. This is all too spy movie for my taste." Jenny twisted her hands under the desk. "Well, you know I have to do it."

"Of course, I do. And you know I'm coming with you."

"This is a bad idea, isn't it?"

"Terrible. But we'll be on the Princeton campus in the middle of the afternoon with a bunch of other people around. It's not like we're being lured into a dark sketchy alley. And I'll bring the pepper spray."

Jenny let out an anxious chuckle. "I guess this means we were right about all this having something to do with the university, or at least the people involved being associated."

"Guess we'll find out in a week. Not much we can do until then."

"We should still look through the department websites, at least." Jenny stood. A week felt like such a long time to wait for answers. But at least her biggest problem was impatience. She hated to think about what those strangers might be doing to the mantis.

Sorrow abruptly surged through her, and the images the mantis had projected ran through her mind again.

CHAPTER ELEVEN

The nice thing about going to a high school within walking distance of downtown was that it made cutting class really, really easy. Not that Jenny had done it often. And she was pretty sure if her parents knew she was skipping sixth and seventh periods to go on a campus tour of *Princeton freaking University*, even though she didn't need to since she'd seen almost everything from visiting her dad at work, they would have happily said yes. If nothing else, it was an opportunity for her to get the inside scoop from current undergrads who'd recently undergone the application process.

But her parents would have insisted upon coming along too, and Jenny couldn't have that. So she did the classic go-outside-during-lunch-period-and-keep-walking-until-you-reach-downtown.

She and Stacey blended right in with the small crowd of teens and parents taking the tour for normal reasons. The unseasonably warm sun beat down from a clear blue sky, and Jenny's black hair lapped up the powerful rays until she was pretty sure she could literally fry an egg on her head. She wished she'd thought to bring a hat like Stacey, whose forest-green flat cap shaded her eyes. A riot of brown curls spilled out the sides.

Jenny took in the strangers surrounding her. Most of the parents looked more excited to be there than the high schoolers whom this was supposed to be for. She eyed each one, in turn, wondering if one of them was the person who'd sent her the email about the mantis. Would they scoot toward her subtly during the tour, pretending to be part of a shifting crowd, and whisper secrets under their breath like an informant in a spy movie? She paid special attention to the teens who, like her, didn't seem to be accompanied by parents and the odd adult who didn't seem to have a kid with them.

If the person who'd emailed was in the crowd, they were likely to be alone.

Unless they're really two people, and one's posing as the parent of the other. But that's too out there, isn't it?

Then again, nothing seemed *too out there* when there was a giant, sentient, psychic mantis at the center of everything.

A girl in a pink tank top, carrying a large tote bag full of textbooks, rushed past. A trio of nerdy-looking boys in ill-fitting t-shirts and clunky sandals crossed the stone-paved path, heading in the opposite direction. An older woman with a graying bun and a flowing white skirt marched past with her nose stuck in a book. Students and faculty bustled across the campus, and any one of them could have been the contact Jenny had come to meet.

She reminded herself that it was no use suspecting every human being she glimpsed. Individuals from all walks of life populated the university. The sheer number and range of people around had to be why the contact had chosen the university as a meeting place. No one looked out of place here, so everyone blended in.

The university's imposing stone buildings, with their gothic designs and old-fashioned grandeur, certainly made it seem like the kind of place that would be hiding a mad scientist or two. Though living in Princeton since elementary school had made Jenny more or less immune to the impressive — and sometimes oppressive — elegance of a bygone era, every so often it hit her just how bizarre a place it actually was, this institution of geniuses. A place where intelligence and cleverness were valued above all else, possibly at the expense of everything else.

It wouldn't have surprised Jenny in the least to learn that the mantis was the result of a secret genetic engineering experiment conducted within the university's hallowed halls, kept hidden from the public but tacitly blessed by those in charge. Especially since she and Stacey had identified two of the people they'd encountered in the woods by combing the university's department websites.

Robert Nichols, biology post-doc, and Pauline Tan, grad student in physics. The bald man and the woman with the brown braid from the woods. If it hadn't been for the mysterious email, Jenny's next move would have been to track them down and confront them. But she didn't want to do something that could spook her would-be informant before she'd learned what they had to say. Or, for all she knew, one of them *was* the informant.

"Hey, everyone!" A young woman with shoulder-length black hair streaked with chunky blonde highlights waved enthusiastically in front of the stone office of the registrar, where the tour began. "My name's Mingyue, and I'm a junior in the Computer Science department. I'll be your guide today."

Her voice was painfully chipper, and Jenny did her best to tune it out as she followed the tour across the campus. Stacey, on the other hand, actually seemed interested and asked a few questions.

"How often do students work with professors rather than TAs... or AIs, assistant instructors, as I think they're called here?" she said after Mingyue called on her. "And what are office hours like?"

Stacey *had* mentioned she planned to apply to Princeton in the fall, and Jenny wondered if these were true questions or to help maintain the facade.

Jenny, meanwhile, couldn't have cared less about the guide's response. She'd probably apply as well, just to make her parents happy, but she wasn't sure if she actually wanted to go.

So instead of listening to what Mingyue had to say about class structure and campus life, Jenny kept her senses focused on her surroundings, searching for anything that might indicate who her contact was.

A scrawny boy in a loud red t-shirt who stared at her a moment too long before walking into the dorm building. An older man in a tweed jacket, reading on a bench along the path the tour went down, who seemed to inch closer to her before clearing his throat and flipping the page of his book. A girl in the crowd of tour-goers who brushed Jenny's shoulder with her own before raising her hand and asking the guide about how the certificate program worked.

Each time, Jenny's pulse leaped a touch at the anticipation of possibly meeting her contact. And each time, she found herself disappointed.

Then, they approached the computer science building, which was in a part of campus that was less concerned with preserving the eighteenth century and more interested in looking like a *Star Trek* set. Glass buildings instead of stone, sharp angles and geometric patterns instead of soft earth tones and literal ivy.

"This is my favorite building on campus." Mingyue gestured at it with a smile. "And not just because it's my department's mother ship.

Let's go inside. I'm taking you off the beaten path a bit, so if you have any friends who've been on the tour, they might not have seen what I'm about to show you. But this place is a second home to me, and I want to show it off." She winked. "How many of you are interested in Comp-Sci?" She glanced around. "You, did I see a hand?"

The guide was pointing right at Jenny.

Jenny's eyes widened. Her hands, as far as she knew, had remained lumps by her sides the whole time. "Um..."

"Yes, I did. Don't be shy." Mingyue waved in a beckoning gesture. "I'm sure you're especially excited to see the nuts and bolts of this place." She lifted her brows.

Jenny's pulse jumped once again, but she was pretty sure her reaction was merited this time. She *definitely* hadn't raised her hand; she'd never even considered computer science to be an interest. Yet Mingyue had made a point to call her out...

Could she be the contact? Or informant? Or whatever you call anonymous people claiming to have info?

Having Jenny come on her tour did seem like a surreptitious way to get in touch. But the person who'd emailed her obviously didn't want to be seen communicating with Jenny. Wouldn't having her right out in front of her, with multiple witnesses to boot, make that a problem?

Mingyue led the crowd through the spacious building, showing off the computer labs and lecture halls, even opening the doors to some ongoing classes and letting people peek inside.

But though Jenny watched the other's every move, Mingyue did nothing else out of the ordinary. *Come on, show me what's going on already!*

Mingyue opened yet another door, this time leading to a small classroom. "And this is—"

"Hey!" A man with an unkempt brown beard, wearing a baggy orange-and-black t-shirt boasting of the Princeton School of Engineering and Applied Science, navigated around a table full of students to approach. "I'm teaching a precept here!"

Jenny stared at the man. That beard looked just like the one hugging the face of the man she'd first encountered in the woods—the one who'd told her and Stacey to go back to the towpath and pointed them in the direction that had led to the mantis.

"Oh, sorry!" Mingyue backed away with a sheepish expression. "I didn't realize."

"That's okay. I was pretty much done anyway. I see you're making a special effort to recruit for our department again."

"I can't help it. I'm biased."

"Well, let me help you bias them further, then." The bearded man turned to the students. "Let's call it a day. If there's anything we didn't get to cover, well, you know where to find me." He turned to the crowd. "If anyone has questions specific to Comp-Sci, I'd be happy to answer them."

Jenny dodged as the class filed out, bobbing and weaving to avoid walking into the prospective students and their parents. A few raised their hands enthusiastically and demanded specifics about the department. Jenny kept replaying the scene from the woods in her head and trying to compare that man to the one in front of her. She wished she had a video instead of only her memory to rely on. His voice sounded the same, if she remembered correctly. And he was about the same size. But half his face had been shaded by his baseball cap, and she'd always been terrible with faces.

"Hey, sorry to cut this short, but we've gotta move on." Mingyue interrupted a parent who'd been in the middle of asking a long-winded question about the department's industry connections. She glanced at Jenny. "I know you didn't get to ask your question and that you were particularly interested in the department. If you want, you can stay behind and meet us at the E-Quad across the street when you're done?"

"Yeah, thanks." The response came instinctively. Jenny was *sure* now that it was the man in the woods who'd been teaching that class — or precept, in Princeton-ese. *So this was your plan. Pretty clever, I guess.*

"I'm staying too!" Stacey exclaimed.

Mingyue gave her a puzzled look.

Stacey smiled casually. "I'm interested in Comp-Sci too." Apparently, she'd caught onto the same things Jenny had.

"Fine," the man grumbled. "But that's it. I've only got a few minutes."

Mingyue nodded and led the crowd away.

The man gestured at the classroom. "Come on inside."

Jenny complied, Stacey close behind, and anticipation beat through her veins. "It's—"

"Gimme a sec." The man shut the door behind them. "All right. Ask your questions."

"It's you!" Stacey pointed one accusing finger at him. "From the woods!"

"Congratulations, you win a blue ribbon." The man leaned back against the desk. "Sorry for the cloak-and-dagger stuff, but I couldn't let *them* know I was meeting with you."

"Why not?" Jenny demanded. "Who are you?"

"My name's Cass Elliott, and I'm a grad student here."

Jenny didn't recall seeing his picture on the Computer Science department website, but then again, a lot of the people listed had been missing photos, and she couldn't recall every name. "What's going on?"

"I need your help."

Blackness and lights and steel...

Though surrounded by forces too strong to fight, the creature thrashed all the same. Powerful forelegs struck at the bars surrounding him but met a surface too solid to even dent. A transparent material filled the spaces of the cage.

Shadowy figures moved in the distance. The creature struck out again but met the same result.

Eventually, though, one would make a mistake.

CHAPTER TWELVE

Jenny narrowed her eyes at the man. Whatever this Cass Elliott was up to, she wasn't about to let her guard down. "What's going on? This seems like a roundabout way of asking for help." She gestured broadly at the classroom.

"Mingyue owed me a favor, and I asked her to bring you here." Cass leaned back against one of the desks, half-sitting on it. "We don't have long—you really should go meet her at the E-Quad in a few. I don't know if it'll make a difference, but I don't want to risk anyone noticing something wrong if you don't return."

"Who's going to be looking?" Jenny demanded. "Who exactly are you hiding from?"

"We don't have an official name." Cass slouched, pressing his hands into the edge of the table. "The prof recruited us one by one to help with a special independent project of his. Picked us because we were not only among the best in our departments but also because we seemed nuts enough to go along with his plans."

"Who's 'the prof'?"

"Professor Leslie Trevelyan, Mol-Bio department, specializing in genetics."

Jenny dug through her memories, trying to remember the name. She'd been the one to inspect the Molecular Biology department's website... "Isn't he an emeritus?"

"Yup, retired a few years back, but still has an office on campus and gives the occasional lecture. I don't think he was ready to stop working, though. Maybe that's why he took this project as far as he did. He's looking for one final hurrah, something that will let him leave a real mark on the world. Everyone you saw out in the woods the other day works for him, and we're all sworn to secrecy. I didn't want anyone seeing me talking to you because that would blow my cover, and then we'd lose any chance we had."

"'We'?" Jenny cocked an eyebrow. "What exactly are you trying to do?"

"The same thing as you, I imagine: Free the mantis." Cass glanced toward the windows, which had thin shades pulled down—not dark enough to block out the bright sunlight but opaque enough that anyone passing outside looked like a silhouette. "If the prof finds out I turned on him, he'll revoke my access, and then none of us will be able to get near the creature."

Stacey pulled off her hat and scratched her head. "I feel like we've skipped a couple of steps here. Can you start from the very beginning?"

"A very good place to start," Jenny quipped.

"Yeah, sure." Cass rubbed the back of his neck. "I was a latecomer to the project, so I don't know all the details. The prof and I got to chatting at a university event one day, and he seemed interesting the way a lot of geniuses do, you know? Had a lot of big, exciting ideas about how living things were designed by nature and how we could modify that. Where I, a Comp-Sci student, came in was with the modeling—programming simulations and such. After a few months, he decided he could trust me with the secret project he'd been working on off-campus."

He paused, scrunching up his face. "I don't know where the mantis came from—none of us do. Prof says he caught him and that the creature was only half his current size at the time. But the man's over eighty, and he's not exactly outdoorsy, so I have a hard time believing he just... went out and caught himself a giant insect of a kind no one's seen before. Then again, if the mantis is the prof's creation— hatched in a test tube and raised in a lab—as some of us theorize, you'd think he'd be boasting about that instead of coming up with some vague back story."

Jenny wasn't sure which version she believed and wondered if there were a third explanation—one that was actually true. "We thought for a little while that the creature might be from outer space," she said half-jokingly.

An amused smile tiled Cass's mouth. "For all I know, he could be. Whatever the case, the prof started experimenting. He said he was enhancing the creature, trying to push the limits of what its biology was capable of. As he put it, he wanted to see what the most evolved version of the mantis could be. The 'best' version, if you will. In other words, if the mantis were allowed to evolve uninterrupted for generations to come, what might it look like in the far future, thousands — no, hundreds of thousands — of years from now?"

Stacey made a derisive noise. "My mom's a doctor, and she thinks that kind of X-Men take on evolution is flawed, and I tend to agree. Living things don't just develop cool powers because that's nature's way. We stop passing on the things that kill us before we can reproduce. I guess you could say we're the least worst versions of our species."

Jenny couldn't help a small chuckle. "Your mom has a cheery view of the world."

"Oh, you should hear her go on about the economy." Stacey rolled her eyes. "Anyway, sorry to interrupt."

"No, you may have a point." Cass shrugged. "I think the prof also believes something like that to be true. He often laments about how living things will never see their full potential because, as you said, as long as a feature doesn't kill you or keep you from reproducing, it'll get passed on even if it sucks. That's probably what's driving him to conduct these experiments... anyway, the point is, the mantis was already as big as an elementary school kid by the time the prof started bringing in students to help, and, according to those who've been working there longer than me, already more intelligent than your average bug. The experiments improved upon what was already there — made the mantis even bigger and gave him what can only be called psychic abilities."

Jenny shook her head. The part of her that loved comic book movies wanted to say, "Cool!" Then again, even in those films, genetic experimentation was almost always a tragic backstory, full of torment and regret, even when it was voluntary. *What must it be like, to be trapped somewhere, with people poking and prodding at you whether you like it or not? Even if you got amazing powers out of it, that could never be worth the trauma.*

"That sounds horrible," she muttered.

"Yeah, I thought so too after a while." Cass sighed. "None of us working for the prof are getting good marks in bioethics. We eventually figured out that the creature was sentient and intelligent like us, yet we continued treating it like a lab rat. And not all of the prof's 'enhancements' are for the better. You might have noticed that the mantis has grown so big, his wings can no longer carry him. He could fly when I met him, when he was about two-thirds his current size. It's all fun and games until you get a desperate psychic message from your subject. He communicated with you too, didn't he?"

Jenny nodded. "Projected images into my head, accompanied by... feelings? They weren't quite the same as emotions, but they were pretty close."

"That's how he communicated with me as well. As far as we can tell, he doesn't understand speech the way we do, although he definitely picks up on some cues. It'd be like if someone dropped you in the middle of a country that speaks a language unlike any you've heard before—Yoruba, for example, so you don't even have a Latin or Germanic base for reference. After a while, you'd probably pick up a few basic things, but it wouldn't be easy."

"He told you to help him escape, didn't he?"

"He asked, like he asked all of us." Cass looked away, something between anger and shame flickering across his expression. "'Let me go,' he said to each of us in turn. 'You're hurting me.' But we all ignored him. As the prof said, 'Do you think a farmer cares if a pig squeals when he's trying to put meat on the table?'"

Jenny scowled. "It doesn't sound like your 'prof' was doing any of this so he could feed anyone—unless his ego's the one that's hungry."

Stacey's narrow brown brows gathered. "What I don't understand is why he's keeping all this such a secret. You said he wanted to make his mark on the world. Why hide something so big—literally and metaphorically?"

Cass spread his hands. "I think he wants to remain in control, and he is afraid that if anyone else finds out about the creature, they will take the whole project away from him. A professor emeritus in his eighties isn't who most organizations would choose to lead groundbreaking research and experiments. He often talks about how 'when the work is finished' the world will appreciate him—and us—but he never indicates what it will take for him to consider what we're doing complete."

"This is nuts," Jenny mumbled. Yet, at the same time, she wasn't entirely surprised. It was hard for her to be surprised by anything anymore. "Okay, so you've told us where the mantis came from, and you've told us that you feel bad about your part in it. You're the one who set him loose, aren't you?"

Cass nodded. "I'm also the one who kept you from posting any of your video evidence on the web."

"I *knew* it!" Jenny pointed at him. "I knew that was deliberate! You were covering up for the prof!"

"Actually, I was trying to protect the mantis. I thought he had a shot at freedom, and I didn't want that shot ruined by people hunting for him, either the authorities because they believed you, or amateur enthusiasts, even if they didn't. Though the prof wouldn't have been happy if the wider public knew about the creature either."

Stacey crossed her arms. "He must have used some really advanced technology to conduct his experiments. Where did that come from?"

"Where do you think?" Cass gestured out the window, indicating the university campus. "He's worked here long enough to know how and where to get anything he needed. Sometimes through the usual channels, and sometimes... through unusual ones."

"You mean he stole equipment." Jenny put her hands on her hips.

"You could say that," Cass replied. "A lot of it was discarded or put into storage, and he retrieved it without permission and had us help him modify it to his needs. I don't think the university would be happy if they found out, and I'm pretty sure a lot of what he did would qualify as theft. Yet another reason for his secrecy, I'm sure."

"Was that weird whirring machine one of your modified devices too?" Jenny asked.

"I wasn't the one who modified it, but yes, it was an invention created from liberated equipment. It uses sound waves to detect objects, like super-strong echolocation. The mantis is already a master of camouflage, and the prof was working on enhancing that capability so the creature could become entirely invisible — so that his exoskeleton could exactly reproduce anything on the other side of it. The prof knew our eyes wouldn't be good enough to detect it if it ever escaped."

"But you were the one using the device when we ran into you in the woods. If you set the mantis loose, why did you help recapture it?"

"Like I said, to maintain my cover. Without flight, the mantis couldn't get far, and the others were able to track him. I went with them hoping to warn him away —"

"Wait!" Jenny exclaimed. "Someone jumped out at me that night. I thought they were attacking me. Do you know what that was about?"

Cass scratched the back of his head. "Stephan mentioned that he was lying in wait for the mantis one night and jumped out to fire a tranquilizer, but his weapon jammed. I'm guessing that's what happened. Sorry if he scared you."

Scared was certainly an understatement for how Jenny had felt. At least she knew what had happened now, and she counted herself lucky that she hadn't ended up knocked out by a dart. "I see. Anyway, go on."

"The day I ran into you, we were out looking for the mantis again. He sought me out and told me he needed to be transported far from Princeton. He knew he couldn't evade the others forever, especially when he also had to avoid being seen by regular people. But I can't drive—have a medical condition that keeps me from getting a license. And you can't exactly hire a taxi for this kind of thing. So, he told me he was going to find someone else."

"Me." Jenny realized something. "You weren't pointing me back to the towpath that day. You were pointing me to where he was waiting."

Cass held up his hands in mock surrender. "You got me. Anyway, that's everything, I think. Basically, I want to set the mantis free again, and I need a getaway driver. Will you help me?"

Jenny's mind had been made up from the moment Cass first described where the mantis had come from. Actually, it had been made up the moment she'd seen him recaptured. There was one problem, though: she couldn't drive either.

She looked at Stacey.

Stacey shook her head rapidly. "No way. Uh, uh. I am *not* letting an enormous bug of questionable origins ride in my back seat."

"Come on, you know he's harmless!" Jenny exclaimed.

"Yeah, but still... I mean... Hey, he called out to *you*, not me. It's not my fault you don't have a license yet!"

"It's not his fault either, and if you keep saying no, he could spend the rest of his life in a cage, being tormented by mad scientists." Jenny's tone grew somber. "This could be his only chance. Since he escaped once, I'm sure the prof and his students are making sure it can't happen again."

"You've got that right," Cass said. "In fact, I'll need your help getting him out this time too. I won't be able to do it alone again with everyone on edge."

Stacey threw up her hand. "Ugh, why am I in this movie? Why is it up to me to be the literal getaway driver when I never wanted anything to do with this?"

"That's not entirely true," Jenny smirked. "You've been interested from the start. Are you really going to abandon ship now that we've finally got some answers?"

"Fine," Stacey grumbled. "I guess I'd kick myself for the rest of my life if I ditched the mission now."

"Yes! Thank you!" Jenny grinned, then turned to Cass. "Okay, then, what's the plan?"

"Right now, go back to your campus tour." Cass looked out the window. "Act like everything's normal. Then come to this address tomorrow night." He reached into his pocket, pulled out a piece of paper, and handed it to Jenny. "You'll need this too." He handed her a plain white keycard with a black stripe near one edge. "It'll get you into the prof's house. He set it up that way to make it easier for his students to come and go. The lab is in the basement."

Jenny glanced at the paper. She recognized the street name. It was one of many named after trees that snaked through Princeton within walking distance of campus. "Just one more question before we go: Why not just tell us all this in an email?"

"I'm not the only hacker working for the prof. I have to assume someone else could be tracking my emails." Cass pushed off the desk and straightened. "Call me paranoid if you want, but I'd rather be careful. I'll see you tomorrow."

With that, he strode out of the room before Jenny could say anything else.

The creature stared across the dim space at the half-dozen humans moving about. The blinking lights, the glowing surfaces, the humming boxes… they all looked so delicate. Almost as delicate as the humans.

One, in particular, held the mantis's attention: the old male with white hair. The one that had started all this.

The creature spread its wings, and they crashed against the too-small edges of the enclosure it was trapped in. It called out with its mind to any that would listen.

As before, none did.

CHAPTER THIRTEEN

The friendly suburban roads of Central Jersey winked under the yellow neighborhood streetlights outside the window of Stacey's SUV. Jenny jittered in the passenger seat, still not entirely sure what she'd gotten herself into. Other than venturing outdoors to get a good shot for her movie project, she'd never been the type to *do things* before, let alone break a mysterious mantis creature out of a mad scientist's basement. At least she'd be up against fellow nerds and not government agents or mob enforcers or anything.

It felt weird to be heading out on a mission without a camcorder nearby. She still hadn't told her parents about that. Which was a good thing since they'd probably have grounded her instead of letting her go to a supposed sleepover at Stacey's house. Stacey's parents, on the other hand, were the "free-range kids" type of parents and didn't care where Stacey was headed off to as long as she got home by midnight.

Behind the steering wheel, Stacey remained admirably calm as she navigated through the sleepy streets of Princeton. Nine o'clock at night was considered early on campus, where the rowdy college students were still pre-gaming for their nights of partying, but for everyone else in the quiet little town, it was nearing bedtime.

Cass hadn't specified a time to meet, and Jenny had figured it was better to err on the side of later. Less chance of being spotted by a passerby that way. She absentmindedly fiddled with her chunky flip phone as Stacey pulled into a street perpendicular to the one Cass had written down.

Stacey parked the car by the corner. "Seems like as good a spot as any. It's near enough that it won't take us long to get back, but it should be out of sight from the house. Hopefully, since Cass knows we're coming, no one will be watching."

"Makes sense." Jenny stuffed the phone back in her pocket. "Um…"

"Yeah." Stacey blew out a breath. "When this is all over, I get the movie rights."

Jenny let out a small laugh. "No way! I'm the horror movie director, remember?"

"I never said it'd be a horror movie."

"You know, 'Mantis Man: The Musical' does have the right ring to it." Jenny grinned while Stacey made a face.

"Let's go." Stacey opened the driver-side door.

Jenny hopped out of the car, and they quietly made their way around the block. Cozy houses nestled amid lush lawns and well-pruned bushes lined the narrow street, which had a good number of cars parked along the sides. Towering streetlights spilled amber light onto the pale sidewalk, which had a few cracks but otherwise was well maintained.

With all the pretty gardens and nice lawn furniture, no one would suspect that one of these residences housed a secret lab.

The girls approached the walkway leading to the house at the address Cass had given them. The two-story home looked no different than the dozens of others surrounding it: sloped roof, brick exterior, neatly cut lawn. The first-floor windows glowed gold from the lights inside, but the curtains appeared drawn.

Perhaps lulled into complacency by the seeming ordinariness of it all, Jenny took a bold step forward.

"Wait!" Stacey whispered, seizing Jenny's shoulder. "They have security cameras."

Jenny froze and strained her eyes to see in the darkness. She glimpsed a small dark device protruding from the wall beside the front door and was glad Stacey had been more observant than she had.

Her phone buzzed once. She furrowed her brow. That meant she'd received a text message—a call would have made it buzz repeatedly. But no one ever texted her. No one could be bothered when you had to press each number a gazillion times just to get the letter you wanted. It was easier just to call.

She grabbed the phone from her pocket, flipped up its tiny screen, and widened her eyes when she saw that, indeed, someone had texted her.

manning sec cams come in - cass

How in the world did he get my phone number? Annoyance flashed through Jenny, but she shouldn't have been surprised that a genius hacker had managed to get her contact info. She turned the screen so that Stacey could read the text as well. Stacey gave her a puzzled look, and Jenny shrugged.

"If Cass is watching the security cameras, that means no one else is," she whispered. "Let's go. What's the worst that could happen?"

Stacey looked as if she could have listed a few things, but she followed as Jenny walked up to the door.

A quick swipe of the key card was all it took to let them in. The small blinking light turned green as hoped, and a slight *click* ensued as the lock disengaged.

Jenny pushed it open and tentatively stepped inside.

A dim foyer greeted her. Light spilled down from the second floor, but nothing seemed to illuminate the first. Jenny guessed that most were in the basement lab. The floorboards shuddered under her steps as she looked around.

Sparse furniture dotted the humble home, which had a fairly open floor plan, with high ceilings and tall windows. It certainly looked like the kind of place where a professor emeritus would live — all heavy furniture, dark colors, and old-timey decor. Shelves full of books with tattered spines, paintings of gothic landscapes, framed certificates documenting Professor Trevelyan's many achievements.

She glanced at Stacey with a questioning look, and the other girl mirrored her expression. She had to be thinking the same thing Jenny was: *What do we do now?*

"Thought Cass was supposed to meet us here," Stacey whispered so quietly, Jenny could barely hear her from two inches away.

"Maybe he's waiting down in the basement," Jenny whispered back. "Let's go… what else are we supposed to do?"

Shrugging, Stacey followed as Jenny tiptoed through the house, searching for the door that would lead down to the basement.

It didn't take long to find the white slab of wood with light spilling out from the frame. Voices floated up from below, along with the humming and beeps of machinery.

A familiar but still uncanny feeling crept up Jenny's gut. Chills ran down her skin. Though she knew what it meant, it was still an unsettling sensation. Especially as it told her the mantis sensed her presence without having seen her or even her movements.

An image flashed through her head: the mantis trapped in a metal-barred cage with something transparent between the bars. Red lights glinted off his enormous eyes, and he thrashed uselessly against the walls.

Jenny gasped. Though she had no idea what the creature's psychic range was, he had to be close, right downstairs.

But what would she do once she got there? That was no ordinary enclosure trapping it, and she had no idea how she'd get it open. And if the mantis couldn't break through, she doubted she'd be able to.

Stacey gave her a questioning look. "Well? What's the plan?"

Jenny thought for a moment, and an idea struck her. She pulled her phone out of her pocket. "The prof has gone through a lot of trouble to keep his secret lair secret. He probably wouldn't like it if a bunch of strangers burst in."

"What—?"

Jenny shoved open the basement door before she could lose her nerve. She marched down the steps. There was no point in creeping around anymore, and it was time to confront the people behind everything that had happened.

Four startled pairs of eyes whipped toward her. Three were familiar—they belonged to some of those she'd run into in the woods. The blond man who'd broken her camera. The bald man named Robert Nichols. Pauline Tan, the muscular woman with the brown braid.

One face she'd never seen in person before but had studied extensively online: that of Professor Leslie Trevelyan.

He sat behind one of the many computer consoles against the wall. With his shock of white hair and thick round glasses, he certainly fit the "mad scientist" mold. He looked far too frail to have been the one to capture the mantis in the first place, even if the creature hadn't been so large at the time. In fact, he looked far too frail to be doing anything but sitting and thinking. Liver spots speckled his crinkled, ash-white face and hands. The shabby brown jacket he wore over a loose yellowish shirt looked as if it might have fit him once, but he'd kept wearing it long after his shoulders had ceased to be broad enough to fill it out.

The cage holding the mantis stood at the far end of the room. It appeared just as it had in the psychic message, as did the mantis, except for one thing: Tubes now protruded from his middle, held in place by a metal ring undoubtedly meant to keep the creature from tearing them out. They were attached to a large silver barrel, though it was tucked too far behind a table for Jenny to make out any details.

A chaotic jumble of machinery filled the basement, which looked half-finished with its concrete floor and exposed beams. Monitors stacked upon monitors teetered over one table, which looked like it had been salvaged from a junkyard. Half displayed an assortment of code, and half displayed images that looked like the super-magnified photos of cells from Jenny's biology textbook. Two large microscopes stood amid an assortment of beakers and pipettes, and a tangle of wires protruded from a box-like machine she didn't recognize.

"You're the girls from the woods." The blond man clenched his fists. "How did you find us? Who are you anyway?"

CHAPTER FOURTEEN

The blond man rushed up the steps toward Jenny and stole her attention away from the rest of the basement. Jenny drew a breath, determined to stand her ground. "I know what you're doing, and—"

"You had no right to come here." The man seized her arm. "Get out!"

"Hey!" Jenny tried to twist free, but his grip was too strong.

"Let her go!" Stacey seized his hand and tried to peel his fingers back.

"Stephan, enough." A low voice wafted up from the lab, but Jenny barely heard it over the shuffling and scuffling.

Jenny tried to resist as the man pushed against her arm, forcing her back up the steps. With a cry, she shoved him as hard as she could.

His hand tightened around her arm when he went tumbling down the steps. She screamed as he pulled her down with him.

"Jenny!"

The next thing Jenny knew, she was at the bottom of the stairs. Luckily for her, she'd landed on top of the man. Unluckily for him, the floor was concrete.

His face went slack, and his grip fell loose.

She jumped up, then noticed she'd dropped her phone in the commotion. It hadn't gone far, though. Spotting it on the floor, she snatched it up. Stacey rushed down the steps to join her.

Pauline ran up to Stephan. Jenny instinctively raised her hands, but the woman ignored her as she crouched beside her still colleague.

"Now, now." The prof stood from his chair, a stern look in his steely green eyes. "This is a laboratory, not a circus. I'm sure there's no need for such antics." He shook his head at the uncon-scious man. "Oh, Stephan. You always were too enthusiastic about showing off your strength. You could have damaged our equipment. How is he?"

"Out cold, but otherwise seems fine." The woman tossed her head, throwing her braid over her shoulder. "What are you doing here?"

"This is wrong, and you know it!" Jenny pointed at the mantis. "We came to stop you from torturing that poor creature any more than you already have!"

"Such dramatic words!" The prof let out a slight chuckle.

"Looks like I missed all the fun." Cass's voice shot down from the doorway.

Glancing back, Jenny watched him descend casually. He didn't acknowledge her as he squeezed past.

"I'm guessing those are the girls Stephan's been going on about," he said nonchalantly as he approached the prof.

The prof gave him a cross look. "You were supposed to be keeping an eye out for intruders. What happened?"

"A stroke of genius, I hope." Cass sat down before one of the computer consoles, bumping Robert out of the way. "Move. I've gotta code something before the idea leaves me. You know how it is."

Confusion spiraled through Jenny. She'd thought he was supposed to help her and Stacey. But he had to have a reason for acting this way, and she chose not to disrupt whatever he was up to.

The prof shook his head. "As they say, genius waits for no one. Now, girls, I'll thank you to leave my house." He gestured up the stairs.

"Not until you free that poor creature!" Jenny took a step forward, but Pauline stepped in front of her.

"You need to go," she said darkly.

"Or what?" Jenny lifted her brows. "You'll try to manhandle me like your pal there did?" She flicked one hand at the unconscious man, then held up her phone and flipped it open. "Let the mantis go, or I'm calling 911."

"To tell them you found a secret lab?" Pauline let out a snide laugh.

"To tell them I'm a minor being held against my will at this address." Jenny widened her eyes innocently. "Help me! Please! My name's Jenny Chen, I'm seventeen years old, and these people dragged me down into their basement and won't let me leave! I'm at—"

"I get the picture." The prof scowled. "You intend to lie to the authorities. That comes with consequences."

"So does creating an illegal lab." Jenny gestured at all the equipment in the basement. "I'm guessing a lot of the stuff down here was stolen from the university. And I don't know anything about lab safety or building codes or whatever, but I'm guessing this wouldn't pass anyone's idea of an inspection."

"You are willing to go quite far for its sake." The prof indicated the mantis with a tilt of his head.

Robert, meanwhile, stalked toward her and Stacey with a menacing look, and Jenny had a feeling he meant to take her phone before she had a chance to make good on her threat.

Stacey drew closer to Jenny, tensing visibly. "We're willing to do what's right, something you guys seem to have forgotten about."

"I thought you knew a thing or two about life." Jenny glared at the prof. "How would you feel if someone locked you in a cage and experimented on *you*?"

"Quite honored, actually, if they were doing for me what I'm doing for the creature." The prof's lips lifted. "I've given it strength, power, intelligence, telepathy, and, as of earlier today, invisibility. I am even prolonging its lifespan. In other words, I am gifting it with abilities its species might never have achieved on its own. If someone were to give me similar gifts, I would be most grateful."

Behind him, Cass stood from his chair and slipped over to a different console. With everyone else now confronting her, he was alone...

This is why he needs us here. Not just to be getaway drivers, but to be a diversion. Well, that I can do.

"What are you hoping to achieve here?" Jenny demanded, knowing that would send the prof on a long-winded spiel.

Meanwhile, the blond man stirred, and Pauline turned her attention to him while Robert stood over the prof like a bodyguard.

"What am I hoping to achieve?" The old man let out a quick laugh. "What does every academic hope to achieve? Immortality, girl! Once I'm done here, once I show the world what I've created, I will be remembered forever. Right now, my legacy is a handful of obscure texts read only by the most dedicated of students, but to show the world a creature's full potential, to give birth to new scientific processes—"

Jenny was glad Cass managed to get the cage open when he did. She'd heard more than enough of the old man's monologue.

The ring around the mantis's middle popped off, and one wall of the cage started to slide open. The mantis thrashed until it was free of the tubes, wedged his forelegs into the crack, and shoved the door the rest of the way.

"It's loose!" Robert cried.

The mantis stomped forward, thrashing in rage. Cass dodged as the creature swept the microscopes and beakers off their table and crushed the computer monitors between its forelegs.

"No!" The prof ran toward him, as did Robert and Pauline, who seized a familiar-looking weapon from a table.

Jenny started toward her, but Stacey got there first, wrestling the woman for the tranquilizer gun.

The mantis, meanwhile, continued rampaging across the lab, destroying everything it touched.

Stephan—the blond man—sat up. If his injury slowed him down at all, he didn't show it. He rushed to a cabinet, yanked it open, and pulled out another tranquilizer gun.

Jenny ran at him but quickly realized she wouldn't stand a chance.

She froze and stared at the mantis instead, focusing on him. "We have to go," she said firmly. "There's no time for this."

The mantis wasn't finished yet, though. Stephan fired a dart, but the mantis vanished from sight, dissolving from view like dissipating smoke.

Jenny blinked. *Guess the prof wasn't kidding about the invisibility.*

Stephan suddenly went flying across the room. Jenny could only guess that the mantis had struck him. But this time, the man caught himself, and he was soon back up on his feet.

Cass, meanwhile, made his way over to Jenny.

"How come this didn't happen the last time you freed him?" Jenny demanded. "How were you able to sneak him out?"

"Simple: He was unconscious." Cass gave a sheepish grin. "I… may have knocked him out, shoved him onto a cart, and wheeled him outside. Another reason why he wanted your help instead of mine."

The mantis reappeared directly before the prof. He raised his forelegs menacingly.

"Don't!" Jenny cried, holding out a hand. "Don't kill him!"

The mantis froze and looked at her.

She stepped forward, her hand still outreached. "You showed me before that you were harmless, and I made it my mission to help you because you'd never hurt anyone yet were being treated terribly. Don't let me be wrong about you. I know that's not fair after everything the prof did to you, but... you're free now. We'll take you to safety. And you'll never have to see him again."

The mantis slowly reached one foreleg toward her, as if to touch her hand as he had in one of the first psychic visions he'd sent her. Then he abruptly turned toward the professor, forelegs raised and wings outstretched.

Jenny screamed, but the strike didn't come.

The prof swayed in place, terror plain in his eyes.

"Prof!" Pauline rushed over to him, followed closely by Robert. The two caught the old man as he fainted.

Stephan raised his weapon again but didn't get a chance to fire before the mantis swiped one powerful foreleg against his shoulder, knocking him into the wall. He passed out a second time.

"Let's go!" Stacey cried, pulling out her phone as she ran up the stairs.

"What are you doing?" Cass called up to her.

"Dialing 911 for real. There are two injured people down here." Stacey punched the keypad on her phone.

Robert rushed forward. "Hey!"

"Hello, operator?" Stacey spoke into her phone as she made it the rest of the way up the stairs and vanished behind the doorframe.

Robert glanced at the prof, then at Stacey, and shook his head. "I'm getting out of here. Pauline, you should too. Help will be here soon anyway."

He walked forward nervously, but the mantis made no move toward him as he approached the stairs. He fled as if he were being chased by a pack of wolves. Pauline hesitated, then followed suit.

Stacey reappeared at the top of the steps. "It's done. They're on their way. We've gotta leave—*now*."

Jenny turned to the mantis. "You can hide yourself now, right? Maybe it's best if you turn invisible for this next part."

The mantis shimmered out of sight, but Jenny sensed it remained near.

She rushed up the steps then turned back toward Cass, who'd crouched down behind the prof. "Coming, Cass?"

He shook his head. "I'll wait here for help."

"What are you going to tell them?"

He shrugged. "Something they'll believe."

Understanding, Jenny nodded and continued.

The basement door wasn't far from one leading out into a backyard. Jenny decided that with an ambulance and possibly cops on their way, it might be better not to be seen leaving out the front. Stacey followed close behind as she made her way across the grass, and the creature's steps appeared as small dents across the blades.

By the time they made it back to Stacey's car, Jenny's face was a mess of sweat, with escaped hairs from her ponytail clinging to her cheeks.

She opened the trunk, and Stacey helped her lower the backseat to make more space. The mantis remained invisible as he entered, but Jenny felt his every move in her mind.

She closed the trunk behind him and climbed into the passenger seat.

"Where should I go?" Stacey asked, buckling her seatbelt.

An image of shimmering water filled Jenny's head, and she knew what the mantis was telling her.

"A river far from here," Jenny said. "He wants to be by the water."

CHAPTER FIFTEEN

The black waters of the Musconetcong River glittered under the silvery moonlight. Jenny wondered if it connected with the D&R Canal anywhere. Even if it did, it could not have been more different from those well-traveled, well-maintained shores.

Though Stacey's car was still within sight, parked at the end of a narrow, unpaved access road, Jenny felt as if she were in the middle of nowhere. Only a hazy sliver of light pollution peeked over the shadowy trees. She'd hoped to release the mantis a little *more* "middle of nowhere" than a spot about an hour north of Princeton, still within New Jersey's borders.

But it was already well past ten at night, and Stacey had been unwilling to drive any further since that would risk her not getting home before midnight.

Stupid Cinderella license. At least they seemed to be off the beaten path.

The mantis, as fully visible as he could be in the darkness, took a tentative step toward the river. He'd reappeared in the back seat several minutes after they had left the prof's house, when they'd still been on the main road. Jenny, fearful of a passing car noticing something, had asked him to turn invisible again, but he'd only sent her images of himself shimmering back into view, and she guessed that meant his invisibility had its limitations. Apparently, it took energy to maintain, and he couldn't hold onto it for the whole trip.

"Well, here we are." Jenny gestured at the water. "Hope you like it." The image of her reaching out to touch the mantis's fore-leg appeared in her head again, and she smiled. "I'll take that as a yes."

"Hey." Stacey moved toward the creature. "I know I'm not the one you picked, and I still think you're kind of scary, but I'm glad you're not trapped anymore, and I hope you'll be happy here."

The mantis faced her and bent its neck down slightly.

Stacey gasped. "Whoa!"

Jenny glanced at her. "What?"

"He... he did it to me too. I... I know what you've been talking about now." Stacey blinked rapidly, her lashes fluttering under the faint light from Jenny's mini flashlight. "That's pretty cool." She glanced at her watch. "Holy crap, it's late. We've got to get going."

The mantis turned away and took another step toward the water, as if agreeing.

"Wait." Jenny rushed up to him, holding up her hand.

He reached out his foreleg and touched her fingers, as he had in the psychic image. His exoskeleton was cool from the night air and rough like snakeskin, though covered in what felt like tiny hairs.

"Before you go... where did you come from?" She watched him hopefully. "What were you before the prof caught you, or did he create you?"

No images answered her. The mantis withdrew its foreleg and dissolved from sight.

Jenny dropped her hand and slumped. "All right, keep your secrets." She returned to the car with Stacey and got in. "I can't believe it's all over now."

"I'm glad it is." Stacey ignited the engine. "You know what's weird, though? These few weeks will end up being only a blip in our lifetimes, and no one will ever believe what we did or what we saw. In other words, these weeks might as well have never happened, as far as the rest of the world is concerned. Yet I already know they'll be among the few that stay with us for the rest of our lives."

"You've got that right." Part of Jenny resented that she'd have to live out all those years not knowing what the mantis truly was. Part of her wanted to continue searching for answers—from the prof, from Cass, and maybe from the mantis himself. But such obsession couldn't be good for her, especially when it would come at the cost of anything else she might have been interested in. Besides, the last thing she wanted was to end up like the prof: so committed to the pursuit of one kind of knowledge, nothing else mattered anymore.

I guess there are some things we're not meant to know.

But that didn't mean she couldn't imagine, filling in the details in ways that fascinated her, coming up with possibilities and scenarios whether plausible or not. And as soon as she got back home, she would go right back to doing that.

She still had a movie to make, after all.

EPILOGUE

Jenny held her camcorder steady as she panned the lens across the wide rippling waters of the Musconetcong River. This new one had a lot more features than the one Stephan had destroyed. He'd agreed to replace hers in exchange for her not telling anyone he'd been part of Professor Trevelyan's illegal activities. The prof, to his credit, hadn't ratted out any of his students after he'd awakened in the hospital, having suffered a minor heart attack. Stephan had awakened and fled, but Cass had been there when the ambulance arrived, and he'd claimed he'd only come by to check on the old man. And since Jenny had spotted him teaching another precept the last time she'd walked by the Comp-Sci building, she assumed the authorities had bought his tale.

The bright afternoon sunlight played on the green foliage. That would make a delightful shot for her latest movie—for a summer program this time. It was a fantasy that took place in a kingdom far, far away, and the M'cong River was the closest thing she could get to an enchanted woodland to use for establishing shots. It wasn't lost on her that the reason she'd thought of it was because this was where she and Stacey had released the mantis the previous year.

Since then, she'd tried to move on, as she'd told herself she would, but couldn't resist peeking at the forums for the unexplained and paranormal every so often, just to see if anyone had posted anything.

About a week ago, someone had. Just one vague account, barely enough to garner any attention, and certainly not enough to be alarming.

Still, you need to be more careful, wherever you are.

An uncanny feeling washed over her, and she stopped recording, looking up with a start.

Across the river, barely more than a shadow in the distance, the mantis shimmered into view.

She smiled and reached out one hand in greeting.

He reached out a foreleg, then dissolved once more.

ABOUT THE AUTHOR

Mary Fan is a sci-fi/fantasy writer hailing from Jersey City, NJ. She is the author of the *Jane Colt* sci-fi series (Red Adept Publishing), the *Flynn Nightsider* YA dark fantasy series (Crazy 8 Press), the *Starswept* YA sci-fi series (Snowy Wings Publishing), and *Stronger Than A Bronze Dragon*, a YA steampunk fantasy (Page Street Publishing).

She is also the co-editor of the Brave New Girls YA sci-fi anthology series about girls in STEM (proceeds are donated to the Society of Women Engineers scholarship fund). In addition, she has had numerous short stories published in collections including *MINE!: A celebration of liberty and freedom for all benefitting Planned Parenthood* (ComicMix), *Magic at Midnight* (Snowy Wings Publishing), *Tales of the Crimson Keep* (Crazy 8 Press), and *Thrilling Adventure Yarns* (Crazy 8 Press).

In her spare time, when she has any, she can usually be found in choir rehearsal, at the kickboxing gym, or tangled up in aerial silks.

artist's rendition of Mantis Man

MANTIS MAN

ORIGINS: Recent documented accounts of this cryptid are primarily in the area of the Musconetcong River in New Jersey, around Hackettstown. Though some accounts place a similar creature in the region of the Thames River in New London, Connecticut, as well as an undocumented sighting in Montana.

In addition, there are ancient accounts of mantis men going back to Mesopotamia, ancient Egypt, southern Africa, and ancient Iran. Some believe them to be gods, others, aliens, and yet others, psychotropic hallucinations brought on by mind-altering herbs or ingestibles used in religious rituals.

More recent opinion theorizes there are multiple mantis creatures, genetic experiments or specimens from a breeding program that have grown beyond the scientists' ability to control and have either escaped or been released into the wild.

DESCRIPTION: While resembling a praying mantis, these have been described as definitely humanoid creatures with mantis features. By accounts, they range between two and eight feet tall, dependent on the account, with coloration ranging between brown, grey, green, and black. Some also claim the creature is translucent.

They are described as having wings, like some mantis do, and mandibles, with thin, elongated limbs and the iconic triangular head with large oval eyes of both a praying mantis and an alien grey, leading to the belief they could also be extraterrestrial in origin.

It has been theorized that this cryptid may also have some form of psychic communication, which is why some sensitives have been able to spy the creature despite its ability to camouflage.

LIFE CYCLE: Unknown.

HISTORY: Most of the sightings of Mantis man take place between 2009 and 2011. The most famous account is of two brothers fly fishing on the M'cong River. The brothers were fifty feet apart when one brother caught movement from the corner of his eye. They locked gazes briefly before the Mantis Man vanished as if cloaked.

In a separate encounter, another individual noted a humming sound before the creature vanished. There have also been several sightings by drivers passing beside various rivers, something that is a bit peculiar as praying mantis are not known for habitating near water, being more common in the forest and among trees.

ABOUT THE ARTIST

Although Jason Whitley has worn many creative hats, he is at heart a traditional illustrator and painter. With author James Chambers, Jason collaborates and illustrates the sometimes-prose, sometimes graphic novel, *The Midnight Hour,* which is being collected into one volume by eSpec Books. His and Scott Eckelaert's newspaper comic strip, Sea Urchins, has been collected into four volumes. Along with eSpec Books' Systema Paradoxa series, Jason is working on a crime noir graphic novel. His portrait of Charlotte Hawkins Brown is on display in the Charlotte Hawkins Brown Museum.

CAPTURE THE CRYPTIDS!

Cryptid Crate is a monthly subscription box filled with various cryptozoology and paranormal themed items to wear, display and collect. Expect a carefully curated box filled with creeptastic pieces from indie makers and artisans pertaining to bigfoot, sasquatch, UFOs, ghosts, and other cryptid and mysterious creatures (apparel, decor, media, etc).

http://CryptidCrate.com

CPSIA information can be obtained
at www.ICGtesting.com
Printed in the USA
FSHW010718181021